UNLOCK YOUR POTENTIAL FOR SUCCESS AND HAPPINESS—THE KEY IS WITHIN *YOU!*

Let Dr. Robert Anthony help you become the person you were meant to be—filled with new hope and confidence and animated by new strength and ambition. Discover *true* happiness and prosperity—as you cash in on your hidden assets for a satisfying and successful career no economic downturn can derail! Learn how to:

- EXERCISE CREATIVE MENTAL IMAGERY to help make your dreams come true
- MAKE A HABIT OF SUCCESS—just by *thinking* success
- PROFIT from your mistakes
- CREATE what you want
- DEAL WITH FEAR—by analyzing, overcoming, and/or using it to your advantage
- CULTIVATE THE *MENTAL ATTITUDE* OF WINNING!

It's all here—and more—in the book you can't afford to miss...

DR. ROBERT ANTHONY'S
DOING WHAT YOU LOVE,
LOVING WHAT YOU DO

DOING WHAT YOU LOVE, LOVING WHAT YOU DO

THE ULTIMATE KEY TO PERSONAL HAPPINESS AND FINANCIAL FREEDOM

DR. ROBERT ANTHONY

BERKLEY BOOKS, NEW YORK

DOING WHAT YOU LOVE,
LOVING WHAT YOU DO

A Berkley Book / published by arrangement with
R.O.I. Associates, Inc.

PRINTING HISTORY
Berkley trade paperback edition / May 1991

The Penguin Putnam Inc. World Wide Web site address is
http://www.penguinputnam.com

ISBN: 0-425-12738-9

BERKLEY®
Berkley Books are published by
The Berkley Publishing Group, a division of Penguin Putnam Inc.,
375 Hudson Street, New York, New York 10014.
BERKLEY and the "B" design are trademarks
belonging to Penguin Putnam Inc.

PRINTED IN THE UNITED STATES OF AMERICA

20   19   18   17   16   15   14

Contents

Preface

The fact that you have purchased this book indicates you are on the path of accelerated personal growth. You can use this book to create whatever you want. How? By learning to produce results through creative thinking rather than by physical effort. Once you have learned to use the power of creative thinking, you will automatically take only those actions that bring you the greatest results. Without wasted effort!

You need no longer be affected by the economy, or any other obstacles that hold most people back. You can learn to create your own environment—your own economic prosperity.

If you follow the guidelines presented here, you will do well under all circumstances. And you will also come to realize that obstacles are actually opportunities in disguise.

My creative intention is to help you realize your true career goals and assist you in making the transition from where you are now to where you would like to be.

In the pages that follow, I will happily share my own knowledge about and experience with taking personal visions, dreams, and desires and turning them into a glorious reality!

I believe every person is born with a life purpose. That purpose is sometimes hidden, but it can be discovered if

you allow yourself to become aware of it, to touch it with
your mind's eye, and if you permit yourself to entertain
the thought of making your dreams a reality.

The daily activities that are meant to be your life's
work are the very things that you love to do with your
time and energy. When you sincerely love what you do,
you will never work another day in your life because you
will feel so alive, so happy and fulfilled, that your work
will not seem like work at all. Rather, it will seem like
a wonderful experience, a grand and glorious adventure,
a creative dream come true. If this is the life you have
always wanted for yourself, there IS a way to achieve it.
This book will show you how. It will help you develop
and faithfully follow a plan for your own success. Better
yet, it will show you why you need never again put any
restrictions on your dreams.

—Robert Anthony, Ph.D.

DOING WHAT YOU LOVE, LOVING WHAT YOU DO

CHAPTER 1
What Are You Going To Do With the Rest of Your Life?

Almost five years ago, I began to develop the symptoms of someone who was dissatisfied with his life's work. The joy, satisfaction, and fulfillment that had always come from knowing I was doing what I love and loving what I do was rapidly diminishing.

As a noted author and lecturer on the subjects of self-improvement and self-motivation, it seemed almost hypocritical for me to feel this way. After all, I was in demand as a speaker, commanding thousands of dollars for every public-speaking engagement. My books had been translated into several languages, and sales were in the millions! Yet, I felt as if there was something *missing* in my life.

People who reach such a crisis point have the tendency to reflect upon everything that is "good" or "right" in their lives. It is a method by which they attempt to console themselves before looking any deeper.

Throughout my life, there had been many things—both tangible and intangible—that I wished to acquire. And I acquired them. I had money, fame, the freedom to travel, wonderful friends, many happy experiences, many satisfying situations in life. Yet I felt that I was no longer doing what I loved or loving what I was doing. It struck me that I must be callously indifferent, or else extremely ungrateful, to feel as I did. Even so, the feeling persisted.

I have always believed that we get in life what we are genuinely looking for—consciously or unconsciously. Unconsciously, I seemed to be looking to change my direction, but I felt guilty about doing this after so many years of following a well-established pattern. Then, too, I was helping so many people!

"Dr. Anthony, you obviously have a gift!" I have often been told. "Because of what you have been able to accomplish, it is difficult to imagine your doing anything else."

After allowing this oft-repeated message to program my subconscious, I gradually came to believe that this was, in fact, my "destiny," that there was this *one thing* that I was supposed to do.

It would take over five years of introspection and self-imposed immobilization for me to break the barrier I had created, but one day, I finally came to terms with an important truth that applies to every one of us. What suddenly occurred to me was this: *Just because you are good at something, or have been trained to do something as your life's work, doesn't mean you must do it the REST OF YOUR LIFE!* Once I had fully accepted this truth, my life began to undergo some dramatic changes.

As someone once said: *When the student is ready, the teacher will appear.* My teacher's name was George. George was one of my readers, and after reading every book I had ever written, he advised me in a letter that these books had had a profound effect upon his life. He also mentioned that he had a "business proposition" that he was eager to discuss with me.

Although I am not normally inclined to investigate business propositions that are offered to me in this way, something about George's letter intrigued me. After laying it aside, I suddenly found myself looking at it again, and soon I was drafting a response.

I agreed to meet with George at his home and, upon arriving there, found myself standing in front of a most impressive residence. I rang the doorbell and, a few moments later, was ushered inside by George's wife, a delightful woman in her late sixties.

George, as it turned out, was also in his late sixties. He had a very gentle manner and exhibited the demeanor of a highly intelligent person.

For a while, we engaged in small talk, and George admitted that he often quoted passages from my books, and that he had shared them with many family members and friends.

After thanking him for this, I inquired as to the business proposition he had mentioned in his letter.

At that, George asked me to guess what it was that he did for a living.

"It's difficult to say," I immediately responded, "although I'm inclined to feel that it might have something to do with mathematics or engineering." (He had four ballpoint pens in his shirt pocket!)

George chuckled. "You're pretty close," he said. "But I won't keep you guessing. The truth is, I'm a professional handicapper. I make my living by wagering on Thoroughbred racehorses."

I was both shocked and surprised by his answer. In my own mind, a professional gambler was someone who eventually lost his shirt. But George was obviously an exception. As we continued to talk, he mentioned that he once made over $60,000 in a single day by betting on a Pick-Six (a method of wagering that required him to pick six winners in six consecutive races)! I was astounded at his ability and immediately complimented him on his extraordinary skill.

"It takes more than skill," he insisted with a smile. "That's the thing that needs to be explained. Most people don't know this, but winning at the races has less to do with handicapping skills than it has to do with a *winning attitude*. What you teach in your books, Dr. Anthony, is exactly what I use in my business."

George then went on to explain that what he was offering me was more of a gift than a business proposition. "The knowledge I possess has value," he said, "and I do not want it to die with me. The fact is, I have always been a heavy smoker and have recently undergone coronary bypass surgery. As we both know, there are penalties to be paid for not respecting one's health, and today, I am paying the price. In any case, I have been a professional handicapper for over thirty years and have made an excellent living at it. I have a son who, unfortunately, has only a superficial interest in what I do. He would like me to teach him some 'shortcuts' with which to make a 'quick killing,' but that is only gambling—and gamblers always end up broke."

"And yet you have done so well!" I said.

"Ah yes, but then I am not a gambler. I am a professional handicapper—a pari-mutuel investor. I wonder if you understand the difference."

"Apparently not," I told him, "but I am certainly willing to learn."

"What I do," George responded with a smile, "is employ *positive expectation*, investing at the right odds, and also, at the right time. It is similar to playing the stock market. It took me thirty years to learn what I know, and if my son were to learn it, he would need to apply himself eight to ten hours a day, six days a week, for a period of one year. Regrettably, he does not seem to have that kind of discipline or determination."

"And so, you are offering your knowledge to me?"

"Yes—only because you already possess the basic psychological skills. Still, before I would share this knowledge with you, we would need to have a certain understanding. To begin with, I would ask that you not teach my method to anyone while I am still alive. Second, you must be willing to dedicate yourself eight to ten hours a day for at least a year before going to the track. Finally, you must promise not to place a single bet until I decide that you are ready. If you are willing to agree to these terms, I will be most happy to share my knowledge with you. I ask nothing in return. As I have already said, I do not want this knowledge to die with me. I would prefer to share it with someone who is able to appreciate all the research I have done. This is a unique business! And while it is not for everyone, I believe you would enjoy it immensely, once you had thoroughly mastered it. Believe me, there is nothing quite so exhilarating as picking a winner at the races!"

At this juncture, I felt obliged to advise George that I had never learned how to read a racing form and that I had always done poorly in math.

"Remember your own teachings!" he quickly responded. "All you need is motivation, desire, and commitment."

I silently nodded my head, and so, the deal was made.

I have since been privileged to learn all the methods that George has been kind enough to teach me. As a result, entirely new avenues of adventure and success have opened up for me. In addition to knowing the thrill of picking winners at the track, I have also undertaken a new professional endeavor. By combining my knowledge of handicapping and psychology, I have begun specializing in the treatment of problem gamblers. The combination of these two disciplines has proven extremely effective. I also present seminars titled "The Psychology of Winning" to both beginning and advanced students of professional handicapping.

Obviously, it was necessary for me to step out of my comfort zone to learn something I knew nothing about. But more importantly, I had to accept the fact that it was not *wrong* to do something other than what I had been trained for most of my life to do.

Through it all, my goal has remained the same: *to do what I love and to love what I do.*

Moral of the Story: Finding and creating your life's work, even if it is entirely different from what you have done most of your life, will bring you more happiness and money than any other single action you can take.

Your life's work involves doing what you love and loving what you do.

What IS that work? Probably something that causes you to experience a strong emotion whenever you think about it. It is something you were undoubtedly *meant* to do, something you know in your heart is the right thing for you to do. Whatever it is, you may be sure that you have a talent and also an instinct for it. And as you perform this life's work, you will be providing a valuable service to others.

Finally, you can count on being well paid for what you love to do. Why? Because money is a natural by-product of doing anything well. Many people do not concentrate on doing what they love to do because they think they will not earn enough. Do you think you will ever earn MORE by working at something you dislike?

When the word *work* is mentioned, what thought immediately comes to mind? Is it a pleasant thought? Does it generate feelings of happiness and enthusiasm? Most people would laugh at the very suggestion of such an idea. For them, the groaning begins somewhere around six A.M. on Monday morning. They get out of bed and march back to their jobs, behaving like doomed criminals about to face a firing squad. Somewhere, somehow, some way, such people have come to accept that work is drudgery. And yet, that is NOT what work was intended to be. We all knew this as children, when we fashioned our elaborate dreams and set our sights on only the highest goals. What happened to those dreams? You may be sure they did not voluntarily die. More likely, they still exist somewhere deep inside you.

DON'T PUT RESTRICTIONS ON YOUR DREAMS

As a child, you did not try to convince yourself that what you wanted was really too much to ask. Why should your attitude be any different now? This is the time to hold on to your dreams. Bear in mind that they won't materialize instantly. You don't even have to understand the mechanics involved in bringing them about. That is the job of your subconscious mind, which will work long and hard to bring the right people and the right circumstances into your life.

You can draw your life's work to you one small step at a time. In the process, you need not take large risks or invest huge amounts of money that are inappropriate to your immediate situation. Each small step will bring you closer to your dream and, in the process, develop your inner resources and resolve.

Doing what you love to do will require that you listen to yourself and follow your own wisdom. Remember, you are always the center of your own universe! Wisdom and power are a part of your mortal identity. Trust them to be there. You have a vast storehouse of knowledge you have not yet used. You have the capabilities and the tools to shape your own destiny.

LEARN TO DISCOVER YOUR OWN ANSWERS

Doing what you love to do is a process of self-discovery. You must learn to listen to yourself rather than to always seek answers from others. Quite often, we mistakenly assume that others are more knowledgeable, particularly in an area with which we are unfamiliar. Although there are certainly appropriate times to seek outside counsel, it is extremely important to develop self-reliance and to trust our own decisions. As you gradually develop your creative-thinking and problem-solving skills, you will find that you are becoming a much more effective and competent individual.

Beware of the pitfall of dedicating yourself to *another's* dreams. Although you may feel obliged to set aside your own life's work until someone else close to you succeeds, remember that you cannot give something you don't already have. Giving must come out of surplus time, money, and energy. The important word here is *surplus*. You must give to yourself first before you can give to others, otherwise, your gift is fraudulent.

Some people have an inner sense that they have much to accomplish in life. It is almost as if they have a mission. Some of these people begin to work on their missions when they are young, while others may spend many years gaining knowledge and experience before any of it is actually applied. If you are haunted by the feeling that you were created to do some important work, trust your inner guidance system and continue to make choices that bring you joy and satisfaction. Doing what you love to do requires that you believe in yourself and that you act upon your own ideas.

Never allow yourself to be discouraged by others who

insist that what you are seeking to do is too difficult or impractical to accomplish. If these are people who have never chosen to pursue their *own* dreams, they can hardly be expected to encourage you in yours. And yes, there may also be some jealousy or resentment involved. Perhaps they are afraid that once you dedicate yourself to your life's work, you will no longer have time for them.

Nor should you let anyone else's ideas or opinions about what you should do affect the path you take in life. Only YOU can know what that path is. Doing what you love to do may be something quite different from what others had in mind for you. To succeed at anything, you must love it, and only YOU know what you truly love.

Being able to make independent choices requires that you take control of your life, that you occasionally go against the wishes and desires of others. Even so, it is important to become involved in the "right work," so that you will not be stifling your natural talents and abilities, so that you will not simply be going to work and turning in a forty-hour week.

When you are doing what you love to do, you will handle even the most demanding aspects of your work with ease. Total commitment will no longer be a problem. You will not be easily swayed or disappointed because you will have learned how to enjoy the entire journey, not only the prospect of reaching your destination.

WHAT IS YOUR PERSONAL BLUEPRINT?

The key to choosing your "right work" is to determine how you feel about yourself, which is closely related to your self-image.

In building a house, you begin by laying a foundation. In building yourself, the foundation is your self-image. Your progress follows a blueprint that you have carefully prepared so that you will successfully attain the end result.

What is your blueprint of yourself today? Does it conform with the person you truly want to build? If not, scrap it!

Think about the person you REALLY want to be, the person with extremely high self-esteem. Such people know what they want because they listen to themselves. They pay attention to their inner voice and listen to their own intuition rather than relying upon what others have to say. They feel they deserve a life that makes them happy. This includes a satisfying job or career.

They are problem solvers. They take responsibility for any situation and solve whatever problem is facing them without waiting for circumstances to change or for other people to advise them.

They are self-disciplined and are willing to work for what they want. They are not swayed by "instant gratification," knowing there is something more to be gained, something more to be achieved.

Compare these people, if you will, to people with low self-esteem, people who will readily admit that they don't know what they want. Such people usually live protected, security-conscious lives that are motivated by fear. They place great importance upon doing the "right" thing, and they allow others to determine the course of their life.

In the final analysis, it all comes back to what you feel you truly deserve. If you feel undeserving, you will unconsciously sabotage yourself if things start going too well. You can easily do this by selecting the wrong job or career, or even the wrong friends and associates. In addition, you will be inclined to place too much emphasis on other people's opinions, especially those of authority figures and so-called experts. Guilt feelings may impede your ability to take the action you really know you *should* be taking. Or you may decide that you are aiming too high and, in this way, severely limit yourself. Consider a situation in which a person concludes that he has no business being a doctor, and so, he becomes a medical assistant instead.

(NOTE: You were not put on this earth to limit yourself or to let others run your life.)

Your ultimate goal should be to find what you love to do and become an expert at it!

At this very moment, you are either seriously or casually committed to personal success. If you are totally committed to achieving whatever success means to you and are able to understand the need to move forward consistently, you are on your way to doing what you love and loving what you do. The big question is not Is the world getting better? but Am *I* getting better?

Do you find your present surroundings discouraging? Do you feel that if you were in another's place, success would come easier? It wouldn't, you know. Your real environment is within you. You make your own inner world, and through it, your *outer* world. Consider this! If you have difficulty overcoming obstacles, it is only because your inner guidance is taking you in a direction that is not in alignment with your creative intention. But once you faithfully begin to *serve* your creative intention, nothing can be taken away from you. Once you apply creative intention to something, you will automatically generate the energy required and focus it on your goal. In this way, your goal will become a reality. In short, if you truly intend to have something—you will!

TAKING MENTAL INVENTORY

Activities you love involve using skills and talents that are natural to you. Your life's work can change through the years, but whatever it is, you will recognize it as your life's work because of the sense of vitality and aliveness it gives you.

What you love to do will also help others in some way because when you use your natural skills and talents, you are automatically in tune with some higher purpose. When you serve others, doing what you love to do, your work and services will be so much in demand that money will literally flow toward you.

Also, doing what you love to do provides a vehicle for enlightenment and spiritual growth. Your life's work will be something for you to think about, to feel connected to and familiar with. It may be something you once considered to be a hobby or the realization of some past fantasy.

Never dismiss your dreams and fantasies as just "wishful thinking," because it is through these very dreams and fantasies that your subconscious mind speaks to you.

One way to discover your life's work is to observe what you love to do and what you do naturally. Also, notice which skills you enjoy using. Everything you enjoy has some potential for fulfilling your dreams.

Even if you do not like your current job, it has within it the seeds of your life's work. You are learning skills right now that you may use later in different ways. If you learn a skill that you love to use, it will be important in discovering your life's work. After looking at your skills, look at your dreams. Your dreams act as a mental model that your subconscious uses to attract your life's work.

Occasionally, your dreams may seem impractical—in other words, too difficult to obtain, too far away, and too expensive to fund. Perhaps you feel you are literally "stuck" doing something you don't enjoy while you wait to do the thing you love. You can rationalize by saying that you will work at something you don't like until you save enough money to pursue your dreams. But often the money needed is impossible to accumulate because of obligations that already exist.

What then?

From my own experience, I would have to say it is always best to direct your time and talents toward whatever it is you most love to do—or at the very least, toward a job that is very close to it. Set yourself up to work in the proper environment, in an environment that supports your ultimate goal.

Remember, the long-range objective is to be happy in your work! Are you moving forward with your life, or just stagnating in a job you are truly dissatisfied with? Perhaps it is time to take a mental inventory of things so that you will really know how you feel about yourself and your future goals.

HAPPINESS IS THE NATURAL ORDER OF THINGS

The fact that people often accept unhappiness or feelings of vague discontent as normal conditions of life does not prove that this is the way things were meant to be. We might just as well say that the body was meant to be diseased since so many people fall ill at various times in their life. And yet we know that the body is actually a magnificent machine that is constantly striving for wellness. Whenever illness strikes, it is immediately combated by all the body's natural resources, which put up a determined fight against infection and disease. From this we know that good health is the natural order of things. And so it is with happiness.

The wonder is that we do not immediately attack our periodic states of unhappiness as diligently as the body attacks disease, since unhappiness is really only another *form* of disease. Look more closely at the word itself. *Dis-ease*. Meaning *not at ease*. There are many circumstances and events in life that can cause *dis-ease*. Certainly one of them is working at something you do not enjoy. Each day that you go back to doing this thing you do not enjoy is another day of *dis-ease*. In the back of your mind there may exist a constant nagging anxiety.

What am I doing here? Why am I performing this particular job? What future is there in any of this? These are good questions to ask yourself, although I must warn you that you may not like the answers. Still, it is important to know the truth about any situation in which you are involved, since once you are ready to *accept* that truth, your Higher Self will begin to lead you in the proper direction. You may be sure that every situation you are involved in will ultimately resolve itself for the good of all concerned, but only if you do not persist in standing in the way of your own happiness.

Just this once, listen to that nagging little voice inside you as it reminds you again of happy childhood dreams. Allow it to talk to you and to begin to point a way. Don't interrupt with a lot of "Yes, but"s:

> "Yes, but I can't afford to walk away from a guaranteed salary."
>
> "Yes, but what if things don't work out as planned?"
>
> "Yes, but with economic conditions the way they are ..."

The standard list of "Yes, but"s could fill this entire book, but of course, we are not interested in all the reasons why you should not do something. We are interested in the one good reason why you *should*.

And that reason IS—because it will make you happy! Happy as opposed to merely resigned to things. Happy instead of just grateful that things aren't worse than they are. Once you stop to examine what people are willing to settle for *in lieu* of happiness, it becomes a really eye-opening experience!

One day, while I was sitting in a restaurant waiting for a friend to arrive, I happened to overhear a conversation in a nearby booth. Explaining the circumstances surrounding her recent divorce, I heard one woman say to another: "I *had* to leave my husband once I realized he had become totally dependent upon me for his happiness and that he was calling this love."

As I pondered this, it occurred to me that there are many variations on this particular theme, many ways in which people delude themselves into believing they are happy, or that this or that thing will MAKE them happy. In the case of the divorced woman in the nearby booth, I could well imagine the early stages of her relationship with this man who was now her ex-husband. Undoubtedly, there had been a time when she actually felt flattered at the thought that he considered her the center of his universe, not yet realizing what an incredible and suffocating burden this would ultimately become.

And so it is with jobs that we take on simply to earn a living. At the time, we do not ask ourselves if earning a living is enough—or if this is even the work we should be *doing* in order to make our way in the world. We just take a job because a job is what is needed.

"Just let me find work and I'll be happy," I've heard many people say, but once the job is theirs, happiness seldom enters into the picture. What is interesting is that the disillusionment that inevitably follows is rarely attributed to the situation as a whole. Rather, the person involved will tend to feel that it is merely the circumstances concerned with *this particular job* that are responsible for his unhappiness. If he is able to find some other means of employment, he believes that things will get better. Why *should* they, if the next job is as far removed from this person's real life's work as the first one was? And yet, that is the pattern that so many people follow. Another pattern people follow commences when they decide that a geographical change is what is needed. But once they have moved to another part of the country or the world, they soon discover that everything is basically the same.

One job is just as unpleasant as any other, if that job does not happen to be the thing you really want to do. You can be unhappy in one place just as well as you can in any other if you are not doing what you really want to do. How many times must you prove this to yourself? How long will it take you to start listening to that small nagging voice, the one that even now persists in urging you toward whatever it is you really want to do?

YOUR SILENT PARTNER WITHIN

The secret forces of the subconscious mind should never be underestimated or ignored. Once they are properly channeled, they will go to work for you and cause incredible things to happen!

The average person employs less than 25 percent of his subconscious power. It is difficult to understand the real tragedy in this unless you also understand that this particular realm of your mind has only the warmest and kindest regard for you, and that it is also keenly devoted to your best interests and overall happiness.

What do you think is meant by those who say: "I knew the answer instinctively!"? Where do you suppose an answer like that even comes from? And why do you think there is always such an overpowering urge to listen and obey? The reason is because we know, without always knowing WHAT we know, that this particular realm of our mind is, in fact, our Higher Self.

In this Higher Self you may be sure you have a friend far truer, far more constant and loyal than any other friend you will ever have. Your Higher Self is always looking out for you and is always urging you toward those things that will make you genuinely happy. Your Higher Self needs but the encouragement of your recognition in order to begin manifesting its powers. Think of that! All you need do is acknowledge what is already there.

You might begin by saying to yourself: "I accept that there is a sleeping giant within me." Repeat this statement several times and notice its effect upon you. "There is a sleeping giant within me. There is a sleeping giant within me. There is a sleeping GIANT within me!"

Your Higher Self is extremely discerning and possessed of powers of great wisdom. Since it can see far ahead, it is able to assist you in selecting the right road, in spite of your own tendency to take occasional detours.

Every time you have taken a job "just to have a job," your Higher Self has reacted, and you have *felt* this reaction through your inner dissatisfaction. Although you may have chosen to ignore the nagging little voice inside you, it did not go away. The fact is, you can never escape your Higher Self, and it is indeed fortunate that you cannot. If you are ever to reach a higher plane, if you are ever to emerge as the person you were always meant to be, filled with new hope and faith, animated by new strength and ambition, it is your Higher Self that will enable you to accomplish your goals.

Beginning today, I urge you to acknowledge this silent partner within, to allow the sleeping giant to awaken at last! Just believing that this power exists is enough to make things happen! Believing is the opposite of resisting, and once we stop resisting, we get out of our own way.

EXPANDING YOUR CONSCIOUSNESS

Since we are all creative beings, it is always in our power to create *more*. If you are unhappy with your present concepts, with your basic philosophies or ideas, look farther, look higher. You will find something *more*. Expanding your consciousness means expanding your ideas and beliefs, and as you do this, you will automatically experience more of the Ultimate Power, the greatest source of intelligence and wisdom in the universe. At every level, you will be given only those insights which you are prepared to comprehend and effectively apply. Nothing more. Nothing less. The principle behind all this was perhaps most accurately defined in a line of poetry by Emily Dickinson: "The truth must dazzle slowly or we would all go blind."

Your Higher Self is a wise teacher, knowing always exactly how far it can go with you, how much you are prepared to accept and understand. Eventually, it will bring you to a point in life that you will recognize as life-*altering*. A moment of truth! If it concerns your life's work, you will realize that it is something that can no longer be delayed. It must be done! The time is NOW! Another dead-end job will no longer serve the purpose. Moving to another part of the country will not make things any better. A guaranteed salary will no longer be enough to lull your back into a numb or apathetic state. Not anymore. And not ever again.

I urge you to rejoice in that moment and to realize its true significance!

At last, you have taken the time to acknowledge the silent partner within.

At last, you are awake!

The giant no longer sleeps.

CHAPTER 2
Finding Your True Vocational Uniqueness

Your life's work is something you want to spend the majority of your life doing. In addition to satisfying your innermost needs and desires, it makes a contribution to the lives of others. Your life's work is similar to a calling. It is your reason for being. You can find it by listening to the inner voice that urges you to do a certain thing in order to gain the utmost satisfaction.

Separate, for the moment, your need to have an income and your desire to do something you really *want* to do. The job market is a competitive place. What you are qualified to do and what you would *love* to do may be worlds apart. You may feel that your capabilities are much greater than your present circumstances. The question to ask yourself is: Can I create a job I feel called to do and receive financial reward for my efforts?

When you begin to focus upon your life's work, you will want to focus on what will fulfill you. A life's work inspires passion! It sustains energy. It seduces you. It won't leave you alone. You think about it wherever you are, whatever you are doing.

When you discover your life's work, you will realize that you already have the gift to make it happen. In fact, you came to this earth with that gift.

Great people we read about seem to have been born to do their life's work. However, most people must search and listen for a calling. You can begin by knowing that you are someone who has a gift within you. You can start by looking into situations that interest you. You can believe that it is never too late to begin your life's work.

AN OPEN MIND OPENS DOORS

The search for your life's work begins in your imagination. Let your imagination begin to serve you. Remember, every idea has possibilities! Every creation has an idea behind it.

The lives of people who have a calling or mission are fascinating. They are written about, talked about, and used as role models by others. You may wonder how they received their calling, how they were able to determine what their life's work should be.

Consider this: everyone is called to a mission in life. The questions you must ask yourself are: What do I love to do the most? How could I benefit myself and others if I were to make this my life's work? You must listen to yourself and take heed of what it is you want and need in order to create the kind of life you truly desire.

Your mission in life is all about YOU, about your willingness to serve others while serving yourself. This is the way that everyone would like to live. You are no exception. What are you waiting for? What are you trying to avoid? Sometimes people believe they must sacrifice their true calling because of family responsibilities. Or perhaps they feel that they have little, if anything, to contribute. It is a fact that your calling will, at times, require you to stand alone, without the support of family or friends. It will require you to search inside yourself, to make independent decisions on what is best for you. If there is a test to indicate a calling, it is undoubtedly the following question: Is this best for me? In other words, will it bring out the best in you, and will it satisfy your desire to create the thing you most want?

LIFE IS A DO-IT-YOURSELF PROGRAM

Being truly alive means living each moment of each day. And in the course of living, you may notice that there are days when it seems very difficult to live life to the fullest. Sometimes these days even stretch into weeks or months. During these times, something inside you turns off, and you are just living to get through each moment. As one thrown-away moment leads to the next, you may notice yourself becoming more disillusioned with life. This is the time to realize that you are *in control!* You can stop this downward spiral whenever you are ready to start living again. You need to remind yourself that there are NO disposable days. Each day counts! Each moment counts! Each day is a vital part of your entire life.

Right now, you have the potential to do more, to be more, and to have more. This is because you have the powers of creative thinking and imagination. The difference between men and animals is that animals are programmed by instinct and cannot reason or use imagination and creative thoughts to alter their lives. So, the greatest limitation you will ever experience is the limitation you place upon yourself. In other words, you can be your own best friend or your worst enemy.

WHAT YOU SEE
IS WHO YOU'LL BE

When I talk to people about potential, I generally ask if they can see the potential in themselves. Invariably, their response is: "I can see it in you and other people, but I just can't seem to see it in myself." When I ask them why it is so difficult for them to see themselves doing, being, or having more, they usually answer by reciting a list of limited thought patterns: "I'm not talented." "I'm just not good enough." "It's too late for me to start anything new." "I don't have enough education." "I'm not attractive enough." Or smart enough, etc.

Each of us has natural aptitudes that we must develop if we are to be successful. Our aptitudes can be broken down into various categories, much as personality or character traits can be categorized.

To begin with, it is extremely important to identify the type of thinking for which you are personally suited. Are you able to think quickly and accurately when dealing with matters related to your work? Or are you more of a plodder, someone who takes a little longer to sort things out, but who always manages to do so with a high degree of accuracy? These are examples of two different kinds of thinking, although one is not necessarily better than the other. It all depends upon the job you are doing, and what sort of thinking skills are required.

Many forms of technology stand ready to utilize the talents of a quick and accurate thinker. Consider the air-traffic controller. Here we have a person who must have unusual powers of concentration, and also the ability to process computer information quickly and accurately in order to avert disaster. Someone with a slower, more methodical approach would probably not be happy in this line of work, although he might do well in occupations requiring some form of scientific research. Then, too, he might enjoy many skilled trades such as masonry or woodworking.

Other qualities that people can bring to a job include a strong capacity for negotiation, an unusual aptitude for scientific deduction, or some form of artistic ability. Some people are especially coordinated or have innate social skills.

And what of the objective thinker as opposed to the subjective one? Each has a place in the professional world and serves a vital function.

Since the field of scientific research has already been mentioned, let's give some thought to whether this is actually the work of an objective or a subjective mind.

Scientific discoveries are generally made in stages. As information is gathered, it is extremely important to look and see what is there—*without adding anything else to it!* One's own desire to see things in a certain way, or to slant new scientific findings to support a personal theory, would eventually prove disastrous to the entire project. From this alone we can see that science requires a great deal of objectivity, as opposed to various forms of creative expression, which may require just the opposite. Consider the artist who is able to convey on canvas his own particular concept of reality. Working from a totally subjective point of view, he is able to create something that art collectors place great value upon, simply because it IS his view—hence, his personal trademark.

OCCASIONALLY IT IS EVEN RIGHT TO BE WRONG

Another thought process is one most commonly referred to as "divergent thinking." People who are skilled at divergent thinking do well in the advertising field because they can decide upon a single concept after rejecting many others that have come before. Being wrong in order eventually to be right is their creative process. In so-called brainstorming sessions, they kick ideas around, offering suggestions, then modifying or embellishing upon them. Even if they end up scrapping the whole idea, the work involved has not been in vain. What is rejected may later be successfully used in yet another ad campaign, and so, nothing is really lost.

How very different this is from the formal reasoning required of mathematicians, who must confine themselves to the one right answer, the *only* answer, since all other answers are wrong. While creatively "wrong" answers can be used again in some other way, the mathematically wrong answer is immediately discarded. *Two and two equal four. Nothing else!* The truth of this cannot be modified or embellished. In mathematics, what is, IS.

People who are adept at formal reasoning are often distressed by the grayer areas of life. They rarely work well with committees, or in any atmosphere that requires a certain amount of "collective thinking."

Do you see yourself in any of the aforementioned examples? Did you recognize any of your own qualities or traits that could conceivably be used in some form of work? Perhaps you possess some of the following traits or talents:

GRAPHIC ORIENTATION—

This is a trait that is inherent in those who are proficient with figures and symbols. Such people make good secretaries, bookkeepers, and editors. They can handle large amounts of paperwork in an efficient and expeditious manner. People with this particular trait usually do well in school.

IDEA ORIENTATION—

This trait is common in people with highly creative imaginations. They are always coming up with new ideas and are generally successful in advertising, sales, or public-relations work. Idea-oriented persons also do well as teachers or writers.

INDUCTIVE REASONING—

This is a thought process that enables an individual to assimilate a variety of facts and form a logical conclusion. Anyone who does legal or diagnostic work, who researches, edits, or prepares formal critiques, is involved in the process of inductive reasoning.

ANALYTICAL REASONING—

This thought process is best suited for organizing concepts or ideas into a workable motif. People who do this well are particularly adept at dealing with abstracts.

DEXTERITY—

This refers to skill in the manipulation of physical objects. There are two forms of dexterity. The first is finger dexterity, possessed by people who can skillfully manipulate the hands and fingers. Finger dexterity would be important in people who do manual, mechanical, or secretarial work. The second is object dexterity, possessed by people who can adroitly handle objects such as tools. Object dexterity is important for anyone doing precision work such as surgery or computer repair. Quite often, a person will possess only one form of dexterity.

OBSERVATION—

Talent for observation is well developed in those who are highly conscious of their surroundings. Such people will notice even subtle changes in their environment and can put their powers of observation to good use in such fields as research, art, or professional photography.

DESIGN, TONAL, AND NUMBER MEMORY—

Design memory is the ability to remember designs such as plans or blueprints. Tonal memory is the ability to remember sounds, a trait that is commonly found in those who are musically inclined. Number memory is the ability to recall lists of numbers and other quantities of information, quite often of a legal or medical nature.

PHONETIC ABILITY—

This is a term that concerns itself with the ability to learn foreign words or languages. An aptitude for other languages is certainly an important plus for people who travel to foreign countries or deal with individuals or corporations on a multinational level.

COLOR PERCEPTION—

This is the ability to distinguish colors, an ability that interior and fashion designers, advertising and graphics people possess to some greater-than-average degree.

VOCABULARY—

The art of communication, when properly utilized, is *indeed* an art. Your vocabulary affects your ability (or inability) to communicate your needs, desires, and feelings. As you continue to improve your vocabulary, other aspects of your life are certain to improve as well. Bear in mind that the vocabulary of an average adult is barely one and one-half times as large as that of a child of ten. The average child of ten knows the meaning of 34,300 different terms, and since his sixth year, has been learning new words at the rate of 5,000 per year. The constant rate of increase among adults is in the neighborhood of only 50 words per year—absolutely shameful by comparison! Resolve to learn and use at least one new word each day.

SUCCESS IS WORKING HARD AT WHAT YOU'RE GOOD AT

Before you can bring your hottest talents into play, it is necessary to get into the game. You can do this in stages, supplementing your life's work with another form of income until you are ready to take the Big Step. It is *not* necessary to burn your bridges behind you, to take unnecessary risks, or to leap before you look. You can do what others have done, and you can also *learn* from them.

Many years ago, a housewife began baking batches of old-fashioned whole-wheat bread for family and friends. Soon there was an incredible demand, and that is how Pepperidge Farm was born.

These and other success stories may seem to involve exceptional circumstances, but that is not really the case. What they *did* involve was a concrete plan that made it possible to advance systematically from one step to the next until at last the long-range goal had been achieved.

Let's examine a hypothetical situation in which a young man has decided to make one million dollars over a period of five years. He begins by saying to himself: "This is where I am. This is where I'm going. This is how I expect to get there." The plan is quite detailed, and he is extremely committed to it. The plan is also realistic, practical, and well thought-out from beginning to end. It leaves nothing to chance, nor is it vague and indecisive in any area of development. Yet, it is only a few paragraphs long:

> *I, Mark Richards, intend to make $1,000,000 within five years from today. I intend to proceed in the following manner:*
>
> *I will start with what cash I have on hand and make ceramic dolls that I will sell at local crafts fairs.*
>
> *I will save some of my proceeds to create a line of allied products including ceramic ashtrays, vases, wall hangings, and earthenware.*
>
> *As the need arises, I will hire employees to make these items for me, and also to maintain my crafts booths, until such time as I am able to open a store of my own.*
>
> *Eventually, I will add three more stores and*

then attempt to franchise the entire operation. I will later add a crafts mail-order catalog and sell my products nationwide.

Once my business enterprise is successful, I will donate a portion of my income to charity, and also purchase a large motor home so that I may travel extensively throughout the United States.

How does your *own* game plan compare to the one outlined above? Do you even HAVE a game plan? If not, it is time to create one, to write it down, and then, to start *living it!* The best way to begin is with a *sample* idea list. Write down various ideas that you have or businesses you think you might like to run. In the latter case, you can prod your imagination by looking through the yellow pages of the telephone directory. From the categories listed there, you might wish to consider any of the following: advertising counselor, aquarium rental, bed and bath coordination, furniture restoration, wallpaper installation or removal.

If you live in a smaller community, an even more enlightening experience might be to check the telephone directories of major cities. The phone company or library can provide you with these. Check the yellow pages for places like New York City and Los Angeles to see what services are available there that aren't yet available locally. In doing this, you could easily uncover a market for a highly profitable business of your own.

It is important to focus on what it is you want to do! Higher levels of consciousness are the key to every new idea. Consciousness contains life and all the *potentials* of life. Nothing exists, nor can ever exist, for you except that of which you are aware. Once you become conscious of anything, you become aware of what already is. Everything awaits your discovery!

PLANNING FOR SUCCESS

Even as you begin to make some serious plans related to your life's work, you should be asking yourself certain questions:

1. What, exactly, am I trying to sell? (If you cannot clearly define your product or service, you are going to have a hard time trying to publicize or advertise it.)
2. Is my product or service something people need or want? What specific benefits can I offer?
3. Who is my ideal customer? (Customers fall into various categories according to age, sex, profession, income, etc.)
4. How can I reach these people? (What trade or consumer periodicals, organizations, trade shows, directories, or mailing lists are available?)
5. What kind of competition will I have on a local, regional, or national level?

If you are thinking of undertaking a home-based business, you are considering something that is no longer a fad. Cottage industries are fast becoming an economic necessity, and while no one knows exactly how many people now work at home, the number is large and constantly growing.

Almost anyone can make a little extra money at home these days, but it takes a certain degree of skill, experience, and knowledge to turn such a venture into a profitable, full-time enterprise. Beginners, especially those who are still employed elsewhere, should endeavor to devote at least twenty hours per week to starting up their new business. By utilizing evening hours and weekends, this can easily be done.

One of the best and least expensive methods of advertising involves writing up a press release and sending it to your local newspaper. Editors are always interested in new story ideas, particularly on a "slow news day."

You can also print and distribute inexpensive fliers, post notices on community bulletin boards, give speeches around town, or join a network of related business owners who are willing to start referring clients your way. Bear in mind that this can all be done on a part-time basis, enabling you to remain gainfully employed while you are building a business of your own.

CASHING IN ON YOUR MISTAKES

Mistakes are learning opportunities. Much worse than making a mistake is never profiting from it.

You can begin by learning from the mistakes of others. Once you have decided upon your life's work, you might wish to study people who have involved themselves in a similar enterprise. You can learn a great deal from conversations with these people, from books they have written about their experiences, and also, through observation.

If you are considering running a restaurant, go to one. There will be a lot to observe and to think about from the time you first enter such an establishment and allow yourself to be served as a customer. If you are displeased with the service, the food, or the atmosphere, ask yourself why. Learn from their mistakes and whatever is gained, apply the knowledge in a positive way once you start to serve customers of your own.

Never allow a mistake to go unattended. Any time an

error is committed, take the time to track it down and pinpoint its cause. More often than not, some kind of action is called for after an error is made. The time to act is immediately! Delay only compounds the problem.

Once the problem has been resolved, put it out of your mind. Nothing will be accomplished by brooding about it. Realize that most mistakes are made through a lack of information or knowledge. Take a good hard look at your product or service and resolve to bone up wherever your knowledge is weak.

If you make a mistake, face up to it honestly. Trying to hide it or deny it will only make matters worse.

Finally, there are often ways in which you can turn a mistake to your advantage. Examine every error you make with this possibility in mind.

The main thing, of course, is not to allow yourself to be stopped by mistakes—nor by doubting Thomases, by economic trends, or anything at all. Remember that your resources are all inside you. Whatever you decide to do, it will not be accomplished because of *who* you know, but because of *what* you know. You will get where you are going through your own determination and skill, by being strongly disciplined and utterly devoted to the task.

While the ambition to undertake a life's work represents a highly acceptable way of "bucking the system," it also places the responsibility for success or failure squarely on your shoulders. You may be sure that the road will be lined with daily challenges and difficulties of every sort. In traveling this road, it will be necessary to utilize your imagination and fortitude, and to maintain an unwavering sense of purpose. Early on, you must come to realize that yours is not just a job but an opportunity.

WINNING STARTS WITH BEGINNING

To begin at all, you must be willing to take that first all-important step—you must dare to do something great with a great idea! Don't dwell on all the things that could go wrong. Every challenging idea invites some adversity, but by controlling your thoughts, you will go a long way toward controlling your circumstances.

Imagine solutions to daily problems. Imagine yourself in control of your life, enjoying constant progress in the field of your choice. Imagine yourself as a person in command, not as a hapless victim who is destined to be buffeted about by every storm.

Make a habit of success just by THINKING success.

Don't let others discourage you through their own lack of imagination or initiative. Don't let anyone tell you it can't be done. It CAN. The time has come to imprint your own unique style upon this world.

DO IT!

CHAPTER 3
Change—Why Is It So Difficult?

The word is *change,* and every form of progress and happiness depends upon it. Change is the basic principle of the universe. Everything changes. Seasons, leaves, flowers, people—everything is constantly undergoing change. The real wonder is that anyone would even attempt to *resist* change when it is so obviously inevitable.

Look back over your life. Is there anything about it that is the way it was when you were five years old? Twenty-five? Thirty-five? Had you deliberately attempted to keep things as they were, how successful do you think you would have been? Would you say that your life has substantially improved because of change? Do you feel you have grown, developed, matured in any significant ways? Of course you have!

Still, we resist change. For the most part, we resist it because it threatens our beliefs. At every stage of life, we would like to believe that we finally *know* what we are doing, that we truly understand ourselves, and also, the world around us. At every stage, we are ready to accept our perceptions of reality as the only ones that exist.

Think of what you believed when you were a young, naïve teenager. Try to remember how adamant you were on every subject, how quickly you took stands, and how

35

ready you were to defend them to the death.

Did you once believe that the secret to happiness was mental freedom? Many of us did. The freedom to act on our own thoughts and feelings, to live as we pleased, to do whatever we wanted to do.

As mature adults, we now know that happiness has less to do with mental *freedom* than it has to do with mental *control*. There is a need to evaluate situations wisely, to make objective decisions. There is a need to *act* rather than *react*, to be totally responsible for ourselves.

When did it all change?

The fact is, you are constantly changing.

Change is also the friend of the true individual, the person who is not willing to settle for what he already has, but who is interested in having and doing *more*.

If you were born into poverty, a lack of change will surely keep you there. Would you rather exist without any options?

Change is an option. It holds the promise of something better. But nothing will change until YOU do. You must change—from the inside out.

How does one do this?

Perhaps the best way to answer this question is to examine the word *change* and address it on the basis of each individual letter. C—H—A—N—G—E. Imagine for a moment that each letter in that word stands for a principle of success that is of vital importance to you.

C—CHALLENGE

Accepting the challenge means recognizing certain things:

- That there are infinite possibilities and opportunities in this life—*not only one*.

- That you are well prepared and well equipped to live up to your limitless potential.
- That you have the power to SEE and the will to DO.
- That you are talented and wise, and deserving of all that life has to offer.
- That your actions are the logical outgrowth of your awareness.
- That you are receptive to new ways of doing things in order to achieve the greatest good.
- That you are sufficiently dedicated and determined to have what you want, to BE what you want, to bring every good thing to pass.

Every challenge you willingly accept will bring about some quantity of knowledge and fulfillment. *You cannot lose!* Knowing this, you are ready to accept the challenge.

A happy and healthy life is one that is constantly challenged. Challenge offers us opportunities to risk openness and spontaneity, which are the opposites of rigid, inflexible thinking. Rigid, inflexible thinking is the enemy of challenge and change.

If you find the word *challenge* a trifle intimidating, think of it in terms of "getting started." Just getting started—moving slowly, steadily from point A to point B.

When it comes to getting started, people generally fall into one of three groups:

GROUP #1—

Members of this group eagerly and actively pursue a new plan of action, making it a conscious and workable part of their everyday life.

GROUP #2—

Members of this group accept the basic principles involved in getting started. They are passive supporters of these principles to the extent that they constantly talk about doing and achieving, but never quite get around to doing anything about it.

GROUP #3—

Members of this group do not believe in rocking the boat. They would prefer to do nothing and to gain nothing. Although they might have some more palatable way of justifying their inertia, it is inertia all the same. Nothing is ever done. Nothing is ever gained.

Since you are reading this book, I am reasonably certain that you do not qualify for Group #3. On the other hand, you might well be a member of Group #2.

Through the years, hundreds, even thousands, of Group #2 people have attended my seminars and listened to my tapes. They enjoy them. They also enjoy mingling with others who are enjoying them. They seem to feel that if they listen to enough of what I am saying (whatever *enough* could possibly be), some of it will finally rub off. Through *osmosis!* They would rather not believe that anything is required of them, that there is any need for independent action.

Group #2 people are constantly on the threshold. At any given moment, they can easily proceed in one of two directions. They can also stand still. Forever. If they choose to stand still, they are still moving, for they are gradually falling behind. But if they move ahead, they are advancing TOWARD their goal, making steady progress, simply by accepting the challenge.

The real object here is to work your way into Group #1, where the real doers and go-getters are. These people have no quarrel with challenge. They recognize it as the very essence of life!

H—HOPE

Hope is that intangible stuff we cling to when everything seems lost. How do you feel about hope? Do you feel it is a necessity of life? I sincerely *hope* not!

The problem with hope is that its basis is in the way you believe things should be. And whenever they turn out some other way, you lose a little more hope.

Once you have established where it is you wish to go, you should immediately give up all preconceived notions about how you must get there.

If you have always been plagued with money problems, then the manner in which you have chosen to resolve them is obviously not working for you. Still, there is a natural tendency to apply the same unworkable theories again and again. Not because they work. Only because they are familiar.

You would accomplish much more if you only learned to *get out of your own way!* If you could somehow come to accept that your Higher Self knows more about the matter than you, that it has the answer you are seeking if you would only give it a chance! At this stage, it is VITAL that you give up hope. That's right! This is the *first* thing you must do if you ever intend to do ANYTHING!

Stop saying things like

"I hope this works."
"I hope things get better."

"I hope someone will come to my rescue
—will listen to me
—will take care of me
—will make me happy."

Hope is a sublime illusion. It promises a lot of vague answers in some far-off, foggy future. It is what keeps us suffering in place when we should really be DOING something!

Hope causes us to believe in something outside ourselves, something magical or mystical that may one day bring us what we want. In time, we become *prisoners* of hope. We fall victim to it. And soon, we are totally hopeless.

What happens then? Usually, some critical change. Go to any crisis-intervention center and listen to the calls that are constantly coming in. There are *so many calls* that later people may joke that when they finally asked for help, they were actually placed on hold! Yes, there are so many hopeless people in this world that hotline switchboards are constantly jammed.

These callers know the long-range futility of hope. For many months, or even years, they have hoped that they might one day be delivered from something that has been plaguing their lives. But it was only when they realized that everything was totally hopeless that they finally assumed some responsibility and took some constructive *action!*

A—ACTION

It is easy enough to train yourself to give up hope and take action. Once you are ready to admit to yourself that you have done everything you possibly can, your subconscious mind will take care of the rest. It *knows* what to do. It always has. In the case of the hopeless alcoholic or suicidal person, it gives them a number to call. It prods them into taking action. The appropriate action. Even *life-saving* action. This is your Higher Self talking! The one who knows what's best, who knows what needs to be done, who knows everything there IS to know.

Think back to any past crisis and ask yourself if you ever acted on instinct or had a sudden, unexplainable urge to do something? Have you ever found yourself reacting to people or situations in a kind of intuitive way? What do you suppose was really going on? Where do you suppose all those warnings, suggestions, and ideas were really coming from? Do you think that they are just floating around "out there," and that one or two occasionally manage to filter into your brain? Looking back, consider all the times that this has happened, and ask yourself if there could even BE that many coincidences in life? And if they are not coincidences, then what ARE they?

I think you know. I think you know, at least on a subconscious level, that there is some powerful force at work here, and that it is always working FOR you, never against you. Only YOU work against you, by refusing to acknowledge this higher source of wisdom and power, by refusing to tap into it, by refusing to take action!

N—NEGATIVITY, THE ELIMINATION OF

It would be totally unrealistic to insist that negativity plays no part in change. The fact is, it is always there, acting as a resistive force. Negative thinking encourages us NOT to upset the status quo. It immobilizes us with fear of the unknown, reminding us how much easier and more comfortable life can be in an old familiar routine.

The thing we need to understand about negativity is how effectively we can make it work FOR us.

Consider a wartime situation in which many are lost because they literally forgot to duck. Those who *didn't* forget to duck took a number of negative factors into consideration. Seeing that bullets were whizzing past their heads and that bombs were being dropped, they correctly assumed that the enemy had it in for them. But as survivors are inclined to do, they were able to counter the negative situation with a lot of positive action.

Whether your immediate desire is to survive or succeed, (and hopefully, it is both), you will need to address a number of negative factors in life each and every day. The fact is, you are literally surrounded by them.

Have you ever stopped to notice all the negative indicators in your car? What happens when you are running low on gas? When the radiator is in need of water? When you are low on transmission fluid or oil? Why, a lot of red lights come on, bells and buzzers begin to sound, and the gauges on your dash begin to give you some pretty ominous readings. Running out of gas on the freeway in rush-hour traffic could certainly be considered a negative situation. In any case, I've never met anyone who was HAPPY about it. But where is it written that we must ignore negative signals, that we can't DO something about them before they do something about us?

I have known many people who end up cursing their cars for running out of gas. "I just don't understand it!" they will say. "Every other car I've ever owned still had one or two gallons of gas left in the tank when the needle registered empty. But not THIS one! When it says empty, it really *means* empty!"

I am always highly amused at this particular attitude toward negative indicators since, of course, they were actually meant to teach and to warn us.

It is important to increase your sensitivity to the negative side of life, to see a need for greater caution and sounder judgment. In every instance, we should be willing to take some corrective action in order to eliminate any undesirable influence. And the best way to eliminate the negative is by doing something positive.

In considering a major change in your life, it will be necessary to deal with the negative urge to keep things as they are. You should be constantly on guard for this limited kind of thinking, and even more important, you should be willing to DO something about it!

The *first* thing you must do is acknowledge that negative thoughts exist. Refusing to acknowledge them will never cause them to go away. For a time, they may be ignored or suppressed, but eventually, they will rise to the surface. Better to deal with them at once and get them out of the way. Again—the easiest way is to replace each negative thought with a positive one.

For example, if you are dieting, don't tell yourself that you are going to skip lunch. Instead, tell yourself that at noon today, you intend to take a walk. Instead of thinking of how you are depriving yourself, think of how wonderful you will look once you are slim and trim.

Where change is concerned, don't worry about what may or may not happen. Think of yourself as a person who MAKES things happen. That's using negativity in a truly positive way!

G—GRATIFICATION

As children, most of us enjoyed a lot of special treats, a number of which were delicious things to eat and drink. As a child, I remember that one of the greater disappointments of my life involved sno-cones. Not that I didn't like them! I could think of nothing more delightful on a hot summer's day than that tasty little mound of flavored crushed ice. The problem was, I never really learned how to *appreciate* my sno-cone, and that was why it was a constant disappointment to me. You see, I had gotten into the habit of sucking out all the flavoring through the bottom of my cone, which then left me with a lot of bland-tasting, slushy ice. I did this because I was eager to get to the best part, just as other youngsters were when they gobbled up all the icing on their cake.

Throughout our lives, we continue to go for the "icing on the cake." We want it, we get it, we gobble it up, and suddenly, it's gone!

We are a nation of people who have come to believe in instant gratification. Whatever it is we want, we want NOW! Why save money for something if you can charge it? Why involve yourself in a physical-fitness program in order to feel better when you can just as easily pop a pill? Why work for a living when you can collect unemployment? Why work at ALL as long as there is a chance that you might win the lottery?

There is something fundamentally wrong with the so-called yuppie generation. The yuppies are less concerned with work ethics, with earning and deserving things, than they are with having and owning. But just having and owning provides no long-range gratification.

Can you remember the first car you ever owned? Most people can, if it was one they really worked and struggled and saved for! It was paid for in cash, and while it wasn't new, it was *better* than new since it was a symbol of honest effort expended.

Whatever you have ever owned or *now* own that came to you in a similar way is undoubtedly something you value. *Why do you think this is?*

Have you ever known people who inherited a large sum of money and who seemed to feel guilty about their wealth? *Why do you think this is*?

You have undoubtedly known people who did not know how to handle money, who had too much of everything, who lived beyond their means, who drank too much or took too many drugs.

In each case, you knew a person who had not yet come to understand how self-gratification was intended to work. An important motivation for change is the gratification of accomplishment. There is nothing wrong in indulging or rewarding yourself for a job well done, particularly if you have managed to achieve a long-range goal that has required much of you in the way of patience, determination, and skill. Generally, you will know when you deserve that proverbial "pat on the back," when you have a right to feel proud of yourself, when you've earned whatever it is you now wish to buy. The best part of all is that the reward itself will continue to be a constant reminder of a worthwhile accomplishment, and that is quite a reward in itself!

E—ENTHUSIASM

Enthusiasm is the most powerful motivating force for change. Enthusiasm is something you may not always have when you need it. Even so, there are ways of generating it, of replenishing it when it is running low.

To begin with, you should *think* enthusiastically. Think about achieving your long-range goals instead of the many complex steps along the way. Think about people congratulating you and compensating you for your achievement! Such thoughts will generate enthusiastic feelings and cause you to ACT enthusiastic! Others will quickly react to this, and soon it becomes a self-perpetuating cycle. Whatever you give out will always come back to you.

Put a smile in your voice and a spring in your step. Exude some positive emotion and excitement and see how others respond. As they begin to comment on your "contagious enthusiasm," you will notice your spirits beginning to lift.

Although your emotions are not always subject to reason, they are always subject to your own deliberate actions. They are strongly influenced by everything you say and do, and also, by what *others* say and do.

The fact is, you have many things to be enthusiastic about. *Think* about those things and allow yourself to feel grateful—and happy.

And there you have it! You may not have known you were an enthusiastic individual, but now, quite suddenly, you do! Well, good for you! Keep it up! And remember to share your enthusiasm with everyone around you.

Now then, what do you think about *change,* the word and the process itself? If you choose to see it as it has been defined here, you will see it as a beneficent influence, as a new beginning, as rebirth!

Remember, nothing will change until YOU do! Nothing can ever be different until you make it so. If you are confused or hesitant about doing things another way, let me make it easy for you. At first, it is not even necessary for you to undertake another plan of action. It is quite enough to cease taking the *wrong* action, which you have always assumed must be right. But if it isn't working for you, it couldn't possibly be right! So, just stop doing it. This, in itself, will gradually bring about some major changes in your life.

If you are presently surrounded by people who are a constant drain upon you, you need only stop encouraging their friendship. Nothing else needs to be done.

If you are constantly obligated to others, you need only stop committing yourself to them.

If you are not really interested in visiting with your great-aunt Mildred in Paducah, then just stop *going* there!

The changes that are brought about by discontinuing wrong actions will gradually encourage other, more positive actions.

Since change is inevitable, you should anticipate it with optimism and joy. It is your only way out of a bad situation. It is the only way you can ever improve your life. You will never be able to make an omelet until you are ready to break some eggs.

Most human beings live the way they *choose*, but not the way they *want*. Our choices generally come from acquired beliefs, habits, and tastes. What we *want* can only come to us through change.

Self-transformation begins the moment you are ready to admit that what *others* want for you is not what YOU want. However you have been programmed to think, act, and feel, you can always do it differently. You can always change.

NOT changing will prove much harder in the long run. Think about that the next time you read about someone being sentenced to life in prison. Ask yourself what *you* have been sentenced to through your own unwillingness to change. Do you like your work? Your friends? Do you like where you are living? And HOW you are living? Are you earning all the money you will ever need or want?

Do you understand the nature of your own imprisonment in accepting things as they are? Would you like to be given a reprieve, a second chance, a chance to make things right?

You HAVE that chance! Every day of the year. Every hour of the day. Every minute of every hour. But the clock is ticking. Time is passing. The years are rolling by.

Do you think you would have been motivated to buy this book if it were entitled: *BEING RESIGNED TO WHAT YOU DO—LOVING WHAT YOU'RE RESIGNED TO?* I doubt it.

Are you presently leading that sort of life? Why? You

don't have to. You can CHANGE it! Now! Today!

If you sense that your habit-infested life is starting to fall apart, well, good for you! It wasn't much of a life anyway, was it?

As you continue to feed your own inner light, a fresh new fire will glow. Once you have caught your first glimpse of what it means to live above your shallow, mechanical reactions, you will feel truly reborn!

Heightened self-awareness gradually brings us to the realization that it is necessary to change. We begin to understand that this is actually an awakening process, a way in which to blossom and grow.

Can you think of anything more exciting than knowing you are on the right road at last? Picture yourself walking along a path of constant sunlight. The darkness and shadows are gone.

Never fear change! Love it above all else, for it is change that will allow you to break through the barriers of your self-imposed prison.

It is change that will set you free!

CHAPTER 4
Your Right To Be Happy

During childhood, we tend to be preoccupied with happiness, seeking it in all we do, in all that we surround ourselves with. How often do you see a child who is determined to find something he can wholeheartedly resign himself to? Never! Children do not like misery and discomfort. For them, it is not enough to go with the flow, to make the best of things. Children look forward to each day; they eagerly anticipate change! And so should you!

What happens as we get older? For one thing, we begin to lose that perpetual state of expectancy. Over a period of time, we gradually resign ourselves to the notion that things rarely turn out the way we would like. While this is not actually true, we manage to convince ourselves of it by concentrating on everything that goes wrong instead of everything that goes right.

Let me ask you this: As you read this book, what is the state of your health? How much money do you have in the bank? Are you sitting in jail or lying in a hospital with your leg in a cast? Has a doctor recently told you that you are terminally ill? If you are reasonably healthy, reasonably solvent, and not physically confined in any way, how can you possibly believe that nothing good ever happens to you? Why, good things are happening all the time! In the lives of most people, the good things so greatly outnumber the bad that they should be dancing in the streets! And yet, they do not see life that way. If you ask them, they will insist that nothing ever goes right.

This is a chapter about happiness—what it is, where you can find it, and how you can cultivate it each day.

HAPPINESS IS THE NATURAL ORDER OF THINGS

If you find it difficult to believe we are meant to be happy, I will ask you to accept this fact on faith—for now. *Happiness is the natural order of things!* Everything else—every other state of mind or human condition—is UN-natural!

If you attempt to test the validity of this statement on most friends or family members, you can expect to hear some very negative responses:

> *"Happiness? The natural order of things? Come on now. Get real!"*
>
> *"If you really believe that, you're in for a rude awakening."*
>
> *"If you want to know what life is REALLY like, just follow ME around for a while."*

The really amazing thing about all of these depressed people and depressing remarks is the manner in which they are usually stated—as if the person talking actually took great pride in leading such a drab, unhappy life. In many instances, it will seem as if people are literally vying with one another to talk about their own bad luck and bad feelings. It is almost as if they are in competition with one another to determine who among them is really the most miserable. But you were not placed upon this earth to be miserable. You were meant to be happy and prosperous and reasonably contented with life.

HAPPINESS AND CONTENTMENT—ARE THEY REALLY THE SAME?

Contentment is something you can feel even as you strive for bigger and better things. Wanting to achieve *more* does not necessarily mean you are dissatisfied with what you have. It simply means that you recognize new challenges, that you see new worlds to conquer, and that you are ready to try your wings. Even as you do this, you continue to be contented—and basically happy.

In order for us to be happy, in order to *know* if we are, we must first attempt to identify this somewhat elusive term. You may be sure that there are many definitions for happiness. For some people, happiness is something they suddenly experience, something caused by an unexpected or surprising event. Many others experience happiness as a result of achieving or acquiring something. Moments of happiness can also occur when you have a creative idea, when you finally complete an unpleasant task, or when you discover that you are able to pay off some long-standing debt. Although happiness is usually associated with feeling good, it is always a matter of personal interpretation.

In order to pursue happiness effectively, it is necessary to come to some affirmative conclusions about your RIGHT to be happy. As a child, you gradually formulated some ideas which eventually led to some major decisions about whether or not you were entitled to love and happiness. In many cases, these determinations were made on a totally unconscious level. If somehow you came to believe that you were unimportant, unlovable, and incapable of any outstanding achievements, you will need to reassess these feelings and come to some more positive conclusions about yourself.

I urge you to accept the fact that you are important simply because you exist. You are here—a unique creation—and unlike any other person that has ever walked this earth. You have much to experience and achieve, much to feel happy about!

Since there are so many individual interpretations of happiness, let us select one that will most suitably include all the others.

HAPPINESS: the freedom and capacity to enjoy.

Whatever you prefer to enjoy in life is a personal matter, but since enjoyment is always involved in achieving happiness, this seems like the best overall definition.

WHY IT IS ESSENTIAL TO BE HAPPY

Experiencing happiness gives life an added dimension. Happiness also provides an inner unity and enables us to move in harmony with the universe. You have undoubtedly known days when you felt at odds with everything, when you felt somehow "out of sync." As I once heard a harried homemaker explain it: "I found myself running from room to room, in a frenzied flurry of activity. Although I worked diligently, nothing I began was ever totally completed. By the end of the afternoon, I could not point to any one thing and say: 'I did *that* today.' "

I have known such days, and I suspect that you have, too. On such days, any feelings we experience are certainly not happy ones—until we finally force ourselves to relax and imagine a better way.

HAPPINESS THROUGH VISUALIZATION

We all have the capacity to imagine a better way. We are free to visualize our environment as it presently exists and also in terms of how it could BE. Negative visualization will, of course, lead to negative results. If you think that nothing ever works out right for you because you are clumsy or stupid, or because you have never earned the *right* to happiness, you are creating a self-fulfilling prophecy. People who walk around constantly complaining about life tend to lead lives that justify their complaints. On the other hand, people who feel deserving of the good things in life tend to work at bringing these things about.

The decision to change your life and to accept happiness is not always an easy one to make. Quite often, it will take a crisis to bring about this change, something that literally drives you to the point of desperation! Once there, you may finally decide that you have had enough of struggling and misery, that you are going to change things once and for all. (NOTE: How you reach that point is less important than actually reaching it.)

Once you are motivated to change, you can expect several things to happen. First, you will acknowledge that there is something missing in your life, and before very long, you will be able to identify what it is. Once you know what you really need and want, you will start thinking about how you can get it. In the process, you will identify the sources of your personal power, quite possibly recognizing them for the very first time. You will also learn how to make commitments to yourself that will greatly enhance your life. And finally, you will be elated with your newfound courage to DO and BE. At this juncture, you will experience new hope, new successes, new forms of happiness. You will finally be on your way!

OPTING FOR A BETTER LIFE

One of the greatest sources of unhappiness is the feeling of being stuck. People will demonstrate this hopeless outlook on life in the various things they say or do. In many cases, the message is tacit, unspoken.

Have you ever known anyone who remained in a job he was not happy with simply because he believed that nothing else was available to him? Have you ever been such a person yourself? Are you being that sort of person right now? If so, do you tend to maintain the status quo in other areas of life—never changing, never trying anything new because you do not really believe that any other options exist? Part of being happy is constantly expanding your options. Yes, you DO have options, and it is time that you began to exercise them.

Most people, regardless of how much they have or how happy they seem, yearn for something better. There is nothing wrong with this, particularly if what they are seeking represents more security, more self-esteem, or, possibly, more freedom in life. If you are always looking for more opportunities, more challenges, you are only trying to keep yourself stimulated in a natural and healthy way. (NOTE: We all need a reason to get up in the morning!)

I have known a number of people who inherited enough

money to enable them to quit working. For a time, I watched them revel in the "free and easy" life, abandoning everything that once gave their lives any discipline or structure. They were learning how to be spontaneous and free. And happy! Or so they thought.

I once encountered such a person in a local bank, sitting behind a loan officer's desk. As I stood in line, waiting to transact my business with one of the tellers, I periodically glanced back toward this person, and finally, he looked in my direction and smiled. Before leaving the bank, I walked over to his desk and sat down to talk with him.

"I'm surprised to see you here," I said. "Or anywhere. The last I heard, you were determined to give up the daily rat race for a world of fun and sun."

Recognizing his own words, my friend responded with a sheepish grin. "It's true," he admitted. "That *was* my original plan. But the fact is, I found out one day I simply couldn't *not* work. And I was beginning to hate Mondays. On weekends, I always had lots of friends to amuse myself with, but on Mondays, they would all get swallowed up in their careers again—all but me. I found it wasn't much fun hanging around the sandpile when the other kids were gone. So, now I'm working again, and oddly enough, it feels great!"

From my own point of view, I could not see anything odd in his actions. In fact, I almost could have predicted them. The thought of wandering from one idle pleasure to another, or cluttering up the day with a lot of trivial activities, is as useless and depressing an idea as any I could ever imagine. The fact is, happiness, to a great extent, is to be found in the enjoyment of pursuits. We all like setting goals and pursuing them with confidence and enthusiasm. And certainly, there is as much joy to be found in the exercise itself as there is in achieving goals.

FROM HUMBLE BEGINNINGS...

Often we hear people speak of their early struggles with pride and humor. Reflecting upon the hardest times, they tend to emphasize their early triumphs and whatever combination of circumstances and events that somehow enabled them to go on. They speak of the sacrifices that were made, the risk taking, and their unshakable perseverance and belief in what they were doing.

In one case, a friend spoke of coming to the end of a month and realizing that, through some miracle, he had actually managed to buy another thirty days. Another *whole month* of working as a free agent, of not answering to others, of being the captain of his own ship.

"In a way, it was wonderful living on the edge like that," he said. "It gave me such an exaggerated awareness of what each day was really all about. Nowadays, I tend to take things for granted. I know there is enough money and enough potential business to enable me to remain self-employed. I fully *expect* things to be as they are. And while I know I've earned that feeling, that assurance that I no longer need to be anxious about things, I must confess that I no longer appreciate my independence as much as I once did, when I feared that it might be snatched away at any time."

There is an important lesson to be learned from this, and possibly the only way you can learn it is by going off by yourself so that you can just sit and think and be grateful.

There is a quiet happiness to be found in periodic reflections, in thinking about how we began and how far we've advanced through the years. As each new plateau is reached, it is good to sit down and meditate on the good things, the many positive things that have happened. Success is an ongoing journey. You are succeeding for as long as you continue to move ahead. But exactly how do you do this?

BECOMING YOUR OWN BEST FRIEND

We're all familiar with the New Year's resolution approach to accomplishment. Whether or not you keep them, your resolutions will teach you a lot about yourself. One thing you will learn and certainly *need* to learn is whether you are consistently trustworthy and supportive of your own growth. In other words, are you capable of keeping the promises you make to yourself?

If you are like most people, you tend to become extremely impatient with those who make a habit of letting you down. At times, you may even openly complain about them. But has it ever occurred to you to number yourself among those untrustworthy ones who are constantly letting you down?

"I am my own worst enemy," you occasionally hear people say, and all too often, it is true.

It is important to be able to trust another's integrity, and it is certainly natural for us to attempt to surround ourselves with honest, dependable people. Still, have we any right to demand qualities in others that we are not also prepared to demand in ourselves?

Perhaps your next New Year's resolution should be to become your own best friend. Imagine having a person in your life who is always on your side, someone who is always cognizant of your needs, always considerate of your desires and feelings. Someone who will NEVER LET YOU DOWN—NO MATTER WHAT!

If you have been looking for such a person in someone else, you are looking too far. After all, who knows you better than YOU do? Who is in a better position to provide you with all that you need and want in life? Doesn't it stand to reason that you are the best person for the job— the only person who can logically be your best friend?

You can begin to mold yourself into that person today by giving up whatever is actually interfering with your happiness. Make a contract with yourself—a contract, in this case, being an agreement to DO something ABOUT something. Such contracts are part of everyone's daily life. The unfortunate thing is that frequently we do not bother to honor their terms and conditions. Successful contracts made with yourself need to be regarded as co-operative ventures. The parties involved include that side of you that desires some sort of change and the side of you that is determined to bring that change about.

A successfully executed contract always includes a viable plan. First, you must know exactly what you want. Next, it is necessary to determine what available resources you have and what specific steps must be taken. From time to time, you will also need to reevaluate your plan, to see if any changes need to be made.

The reason most people fail to honor the contracts they hold with themselves is that "living is so daily." If we could decide upon a course of action and then execute it in a relatively short period of time, we would be more inclined to see the matter through. As it is, the days stretch into weeks, the weeks into months, and the months into years. During that time, we have many opportunities to backtrack on or even abandon our dreams and, very often, we do. And, of course, we are always *unhappy* when we do.

The next time you experience a feeling of utter disgust because you cannot seem to honor your contracts with yourself, I would urge you to remember that feeling. Notice the depression and misery it causes. Then think about whether you really can afford to be affected this way. The only logical alternative, of course, is to replace your negative habits with positive ones.

If you find it difficult to stick with your resolutions, then it is time to look at your options. Yes, you DO have options, in all matters great and small.

Let us consider for a moment the dilemma of a young career woman who has become chronically negligent in her household chores.

"I can't afford a maid," she admits, "but even if I could, there isn't that much to clean. Once I make up my mind to do it, I can clean the entire place in about four hours. But I find it so difficult to get started. The real problem is that I am basically an immaculate person. I dearly love to have everything in its place. And because of this, it is extremely hard for me to live amid constant clutter and chaos. Yet I continue to do it. I simply *hate* housework, but I hate not being able to discipline myself even more. Lately, I've begun to feel terribly depressed."

In dealing with this hypothetical situation, my first impulse would be to suggest to this woman that she confront the issue and deal with it in the same way that she would deal with a problem at work.

Assuming her company had recently adopted a major reorganization plan, I might be inclined to ask her how it had been facilitated, over what period of time, and how successful it actually was.

As we all know, reorganization plans can create chaos unless they are gradually phased in as the older, more obsolete plan is being phased out. One way in which a new plan can be effectively adopted is through the concept of "one department at a time."

Applying this same philosophy to housework, it might be best to suggest to this woman that she make a point of thoroughly cleaning one room of her home each day. In that way, she will never have the entire house to clean, and it will always look good with a minimum of daily effort.

Options! Yes, you always have options, and once you begin to exercise them, think how good you will feel at having gained control over a situation that once controlled you!

With most people, it is the little everyday things that tend to get them down. The major problems and crises are invariably attended to, because there is such an urgency about them. But other things, the things that tend to cause a nagging discontent, are usually ignored until our self-esteem begins to suffer because we are unwilling to deal with the issues at hand.

A CELEBRATION OF LIFE

How much better it is to live in such a way that you can celebrate life! And so you should! There are many causes for celebration, and you will discover them easily enough, if you only look!

Right now, you have good reason to celebrate your pursuit of happiness, your overall enjoyment of life, your freedom to think and act and be what you choose. If you would like to make it a real party, send out formal invitations! In addition to the date, time, and place, state the reason for your celebration, the goal you have reached in your action-based program for happiness, and assure your guests that you are looking forward to their attendance because their presence will enhance your life!

Let others confine themselves to the more customary reasons for celebration—the major holidays that are familiar to us all. If that is all people can think to celebrate, what are they really telling you? What they are saying is that they must rely on some outside influence to get them in the mood to celebrate. Until merchants start advertising their sales, ringing their bells, and piping in the appropriate music, there is nothing for them to feel happy or festive about. Do you agree with that? I sincerely hope not!

It is not through our acquisition of material things but rather through our *capacity to enjoy* that we know true happiness. If you are gradually losing your capacity to enjoy, you must make every effort to revive it. Think back to your childhood days and how keenly you enjoyed things then. Little things. Simple things. The sound of an ice-cream truck coming down the street. A huge pile of autumn leaves to play in. A day at the park. A Saturday matinee. A bag of freshly roasted peanuts. A good book to read.

The point I am trying to make is that there is much happiness to be found wherever you look. But first, you must look. Look as a child would look, with that simple, childlike wonder.

More than a thousand years ago, the mighty Caliph of Cordova wrote:

> *I have now reigned above fifty years in victory or peace, beloved by my subjects, dreaded by my enemies, and respected by my allies. Riches and honors, power and pleasure, have waited on my call, nor does any earthly blessing appear to have been wanting to my felicity. In this situation I have diligently numbered the days of pure and genuine happiness which have fallen to my lot. They amount to fourteen.*

Although success and happiness are frequently equated, as if the attainment of the first automatically guaranteed the second, we know this is not really true. If it were, all wealthy and professionally successful people would be deliriously happy and, of course, they are not. There is no happiness to be experienced unless there is first a capacity for enjoyment. And for that, you must go back in time, you must remember life's simpler pleasures and the manner in which you were once able to appreciate them.

You have not lost your capacity to enjoy; you have misplaced it. You can find it again by giving yourself a chance to achieve, to *create* something, and to acknowledge honestly what it is that you have done!

It is important that you take your rightful place in this world, knowing it IS your place and no one else's.

Strive to enjoy honorable and pleasant relations with those around you.

You may be sure that your plans, hopes, and dreams are all part of the daily food and drink you require to survive. They are essential to your good health and well-being. It is not enough to exist—to put in your time on this earth. You are here for a reason! There is something you need to accomplish. I urge you to begin today—to look to your dreams and become what you have always wanted to be. And through it all, remember always to be loyal and true to yourself, and also, to *be happy!*

CHAPTER 5
Turning On Your Dream Machine

You are undoubtedly familiar with the old adage: *Seeing is believing.* Had you ever stopped to think that the reverse might also be true? *Believing is seeing.* Until you are able to see the things you want, really SEE them through a process known as Creative Mental Imagery, it will be difficult for you to generate enough energy, desire, or enthusiasm to bring these things into your life.

If you were to ask the average person what he really wants out of life, he would inundate you with a lot of vague answers: "A bigger house." "A better job." "More money." "Less tension and stress." "A place to get away from it all."

Do you see anything wrong with these answers? Probably not, if you have been thinking along the same lines. But there is a problem with these desires. The problem is that you don't want anything really *specific.* Do you think you are asking for something specific when you ask for a bigger house? What kind of house? Where is it located? How many rooms does it have? What price range is it in?

And what about more money? How much money is "more"? Five thousand dollars? Fifty thousand? A million?

And finally, this business about a better job. What kind of job would you like? Doing what, and for what salary?

Are you beginning to see the problem with nonspecific goals? How can your subconscious mind possibly go to work on them? Your subconscious is a powerful tool and will work long and hard to help you achieve what you want—but only after it has been given specific instructions!

TURN ON YOUR DREAM MACHINE

The first step toward getting what you really want in life is to allow yourself to dream. Every time you dream of something that you want, you are forming a part of your future. There is great power in reviewing your dreams over and over again. Think about the things you already have and ask yourself how you actually achieved them. Isn't it true that you carried some very strong pictures of your goals in your mind throughout the time you were working toward them?

Your imagination is your direct link to your innermost desires. It is not bound by your habits, beliefs, or inner fears. The Creator provided you with the gift of imagination to allow you to transcend the limitations of your past, present, and future. Imagination gives you the ability to step outside of your self-imposed limitations and create new and unlimited possibilities. When you think about what you want to achieve, try to picture the best possible outcome to the situation. To increase your ability to turn your desires into reality, push yourself to imagine an even better outcome than the one you originally perceived. Every time you imagine something, see if you can make it even bigger and better! Dare to go beyond the boundaries you have always set for yourself. *Enlarge* the picture and play with new ideas.

When you do this, you may find that your less specific, less imaginative desires are still creating your present reality. Don't be discouraged! Gradually, your old thought patterns will be replaced by new and challenging ideas.

Through the years, I have known people in many walks of life. Some were able to achieve their desires, and many others were not. In one case, a man I spoke with was a long-distance driver employed by a major trucking company. His dream was to one day own a truck of his own and to operate independently. We talked of many things in a general way, but then got down to specifics.

"Assuming you had the money," I said, "do you know what kind of truck you'd like to own?"

At that, the man grinned and his eyes began to sparkle. "Do I *know?*" he said. "Why, I've thought of nothing else! It's a long-nosed Peterbilt with a four-and-a-quarter Caterpillar engine. Fifteen forward speeds. Bridgestone tires all around. Air-ride suspension, stereo AM/FM cassette player, a built-in clock radio, wood-grain dash, sheepskin seat covers, and a sixty-inch Aerodyne sleeper."

"What color is it?" I asked, and then smiled at his ready response.

"Black. With silver trim."

By the time we were finished talking, I was able to envision this man's truck as clearly as he was able to envision it himself. And one day, a couple of years later, I actually *saw* the truck, and it was exactly as its owner had described it.

"Well, what do you think?" he asked excitedly as he continued to circle this huge, handsome rig.

"I think I knew about this day two years ago," I told him. "I knew it would happen, Jerry. I knew you wouldn't fail."

If I were to ask you today, *this moment*, to describe the

next house you would like to live in, the next car you would like to drive—in *intricate detail*, as intricately as my truck-driver friend was able to describe his truck—do you think that you could? I have no doubt that you could do it eventually, but do you think you could do it right now?

How about your life's work? Do you have a concrete plan for doing whatever it is you would really like to do? Do you know exactly how you will begin, how you intend to develop and expand? Have you thought about how much you will be earning five, ten, even twenty years from now? Have you thought about potentially successful offshoots of your work, other areas in which you might care to branch out?

It's a lot to think about, isn't it? It's a lot to think about and visualize, but *visualize* it you must! Nothing will happen until you accept that "believing is seeing."

WHAT WAS THAT AGAIN?

It is unfortunate that so many clichés are automatically accepted as truths. "Seeing is believing" is certainly one of those clichés. Do you suppose we ever would have had an opportunity to enjoy all the great inventions in this world if the inventors had limited themselves to believing only in those things that already existed? If we are to prosper and grow, we must let our imaginations take us beyond what can only be seen with our eyes. You will start to move ahead toward your goal when you believe in it so strongly that you can see it through Creative Mental Imagery. Believing is seeing!

Another unfortunate cliché is "back and forth." Here is a phrase that actually assumes you can go *back* before you have even *been* anywhere! To be more accurate, shouldn't we really be saying "forth and back"? First we go ahead—then we move back. Unless, of course, you are more interested in constantly moving forward. In that case, you must first face up to the fact that having what you want is important enough to warrant some genuine effort.

NO MORE HOCUS-POCUS—ONLY FOCUS

Once you really *zero in* on a goal—and Creative Mental Imagery will enable you to do that—you can focus all of your thoughts and energies on it. The power you will generate can best be described by the following analogy: Let's say you open a shotgun shell and spill the powder out on the table. If you strike a match to it, it will burn harmlessly. If you blow or sneeze at it, it will quickly be dispersed in a harmless cloud. Yet, if you take that same amount of powder and return it to the shell, then place the shell in a gun and aim it at a target, you now have a *powerful weapon!*

Zeroing in on your goal and concentrating only on IT is what makes achieving it possible. This is the reason why people often work best in crisis situations. During ordinary times, these same people may divide up their talents and personal power, going off in too many directions at once—in other words, scattering their shot. But once a crisis enters their lives, everything changes. The reason for this is that a crisis narrows their choices. Yet, crisis itself has no power. It merely forces people to focus on a single thing—to concentrate all of their strengths and energies on a single target. In that sense, a crisis literally compels you to do the thing you should have been doing all along.

Think of something you want right now. (Specifically,

please!) Do you really intend to have it, or are you merely wishing or hoping that it will eventually come your way?

How much time do you actually devote to thinking about your dreams in the interest of making them a reality? Do you often find yourself preoccupied, even obsessed, with them? Good! Nothing will happen unless your dreams are extremely important to you.

Think of something in your life that came about because of your adamant determination to have it. There were undoubtedly obstacles in your path, and yet you effectively overcame them. You just wouldn't take no for an answer. In your own mind, there simply wasn't any way that you were going to sacrifice your creative intention, and because of this, you ultimately realized your goal.

Once you master the process of creating from thought, you will no longer be imprisoned by any outside circumstance or condition. You will be able to create the appropriate atmosphere for accomplishment, and you will do this by gradually altering your thought patterns and expanding your belief system to a point where you feel truly entitled to whatever it is you want.

Everything around you once existed as a thought in someone's mind. Your car. Your home. Your clothes. Even the community you live in. Each and every one of these things began as an idea in someone's mind. They all existed as thoughts before becoming reality.

Your thoughts set up the model of what is to be created. Your emotions then energize your thoughts, which, in turn, motivate you to take action. The stronger your convictions and emotions, the more rapidly you will achieve your aims. Your intention to act both fuels and directs your thoughts, enabling you to maintain a steady focus on what you want until you actually obtain it.

CREATIVE MENTAL IMAGERY AT WORK

We move toward what we think about—and VISU-ALIZE! Physically, emotionally, and psychologically, we create through activity and movement whatever we hold as a clear and compelling picture in our minds. As long as we hold that picture, we are drawn to it! A mental picture is a scene played out upon the screen of your mind. The entire thinking process is, in large measure, a projection of mental scenes. First this scene, then that, then the next.

In chapter two of this book you learned how an industrious young man by the name of Mark Richards decided to earn a million dollars. He did not simply wish for such an amount or conclude that it would be nice to have it. He invented an actual step-by-step plan that was both logical and feasible. And the individual steps involved were never beyond his capabilities, which is an important thing to consider when making plans of your own.

Each day, picture something that you can accomplish in the process of working toward your goal. Picture it clearly. Imagine yourself doing it. Then, execute it faithfully. Many people find it helpful to compile a Scrapbook of Dreams. It's simple to make, and incidentally, it is also a great deal of fun!

Look through magazines and newspapers for pictures, words, and sentences related to those things you wish to achieve, and cut them out. Paste a picture of the home you have always wanted on a large sheet of construction paper. Outside the house, paste a picture of a car you would like to drive. Somewhere nearby, paste a picture of your place of employment, with the name of the business boldly printed across the front. As you do these things, imagine yourself living in the house of your dreams, walking through its rooms, arranging its furniture, enjoying its warm and cozy atmosphere. Imagine yourself walking out of this house, sliding behind the wheel of your car, and driving off to work. Imagine the workplace of your dreams, with an office as you would like it arranged, with friendly and faithful customers wandering in and out. Is the picture becoming clearer? Are you becoming more interested and enthused?

You may be sure that this is not *all* that is happening. Throughout the entire time that your Creative Mental Imagery is at work, the power of your mind will also be drawing these things to you. Your Scrapbook of Dreams is a means of impressing upon your subconscious mind the pattern from which you intend to create success and harmony. The dreams are specific—fully detailed. Even the shapes and colors of things are there. Remember the man with the truck? Black with silver trim. Not a white truck, or a green one. Not any old truck at all. No, the subconscious mind doesn't know how to work with "any old truck at all." Or any old *thought* at all. And it can *never* work unless there is a picture!

If you have never trained yourself to visualize things, I urge you to begin at once. There are many ways in which you can do this.

Tomorrow, as you read the morning paper, take the time to envision the events you are reading about. If you are reading about a fire, close your eyes and imagine the flames, the heat, the smoke, and the firemen and all their equipment. Think about the experience of fighting and also surviving such a blaze, and let these pictures run freely through your mind. At first, you may only see a faint image. A vague picture or two. But soon there will be others, each stronger and clearer than the last. Before very long, you will find yourself *reacting* as your emotions become involved. This is how visualization works with your own desires and goals. The picture of your goal generates emotional reactions.

THERE IS MOTION IN *E-MOTION*

Can you remember where you were and what you were doing on the day of President Kennedy's assassination? Many people are able to tell you every detail of that day, even down to the clothes they were wearing. In this particular instance, our memories (or mental pictures) are strongly infused with *emotion*. It is the emotion involved that makes the scene so real to us—and so it is with visualization.

Once you are able to form a clear picture of what you want, your emotions come into play. They begin to react to the dream as if it were full-blown reality. *Your subconscious mind does not know the difference!* It responds to whatever you feed it, to whatever you tell it is true. Think about that—about the POWER in that!

What images immediately come to mind when I mention the words *home, car, work, bank account*, and *friends*? I would venture to say that you probably see things as they are, not as you would like for them to be. Perhaps you believe this to be only practical or realistic. After all, this IS your house, this IS your car, and you only have so much money in the bank. What is the sense in pretending? Ah yes, but I am not asking you to *pretend*. I am asking you to accept the fact that believing is seeing—that you can have the things you *visualize*—and that you will never have them any other way.

YOUR LIFE IS THE RESULT OF HOW YOU SEE LIFE

Suppose you are about to walk out on a stage to address an auditorium filled with people. Just before you do, a mental picture comes into your mind of how it was the last time you did this. You were nervous and uncertain. You felt suddenly unprepared. You could not believe that anything you had to say would prove to be of any interest. As you play back this picture, what happens? You begin to experience the same nervousness, uncertainty, and doubt. Your past viewpoint has now become your *present* viewpoint, and you are destined to fail again.

Do you believe that last statement? Why? What if I were to ask you to take that mental picture of the past and to smash it to smithereens. Forbid yourself to be governed by the past. This is a new situation. A new audience. A new opportunity for you to excel.

Picture yourself striding out on that stage with great confidence and poise. You have come to speak on a topic you know well. You are well prepared. It is a subject you have researched and thoroughly studied. No one is a better authority. Today, you have something useful and important to say, and hundreds are waiting to hear you. They wish to avail themselves of the information you have to impart. They are eager for you to begin!

When picturing yourself in this new light, how do you find yourself reacting? Are your nerves a bit calmer? Do you feel stronger, more confident, and ready to go on stage? Good! That is how you *should* feel!

Throughout your life, you should always feel ready to go on stage, to perform with confidence and pride, to be the star of your own show. But first, you must SEE yourself in that role. Yes, I know it is hard. I also know *why* it is hard. And that is something else that needs to be discussed.

Let us assume that you are a taxi driver who would one day like to be an engineer. Or a store clerk who would one day like to be a doctor. Even as you read these words, you may be sure there are thousands of people doing *one* thing and secretly wishing they could be doing *something else!* I have spoken with a number of them, and not surprisingly, they often seem downcast.

"Each day," they tell me, "I seem to get farther and farther away from my goal. I know what I want to do, and I have a clear picture of it, too! But I also have a clear picture of all the bills that need to be paid, and I know I need a job. The job I presently have isn't really the one I want, but it's something I *have* to do! At least for now. While I'm working toward my dream."

There is nothing wrong with having to do one thing while dreaming of doing another, as long as you have learned the proper way to feel about it.

"Bad! I feel *bad!*" I once heard someone say. "I'm a shoe salesman and I want to be a writer! But nothing is working out."

Employing the art of Creative Mental Imagery, I urged this person to see his circumstances in a slightly different way. "As it is," I said, "you see yourself as a shoe salesman who would one day like to be a writer. Why not think of yourself as a writer who is temporarily working as a shoe salesman?"

As this alternate way of thinking began to register in this person's mind, I saw an immediate reaction on his face. All in a moment, he appeared happier and calmer and more optimistic about things.

Do you see how important it is to *identify* with what it is you really want? Not with what you have—but with what you SEE IN YOUR MIND?

YOU RECEIVE WHAT YOU PERCEIVE

New mental pictures mean a wonderful new life! They give our ideas power. Seeing something will eventually enable you to *have* it since your level of mental awareness automatically attracts a corresponding way of life. It is important to see that there are different levels of awareness. On the lowest level, we are concerned with everyday survival. Food, clothing, and shelter—nothing more. If you were to offer a starving, homeless person a trip to Paris, France, it would prove of little interest. And in his immediate situation, you could certainly see why. When we are hungry and homeless, it is difficult to think beyond that. But once these needs have been satisfied, it is quite natural to want something more.

As your level of awareness gradually expands, you begin to think in terms of achievement and success. You begin to *identify* with such things, to see yourself functioning happily and efficiently in a life that is presently a dream.

A CREATIVE MENTAL IMAGERY PARTY

Most people like to give parties and also go to them. New Year's Eve parties, birthday, anniversary, even Halloween parties. Although there are parties galore, I see the need for yet another one—a different sort of party, with a highly unusual theme!

What would you think of hosting or attending a Creative Mental Imagery party? Here is how it would work: To begin with, we would invite only creative and independent thinkers, people with bright ideas and bold dreams, who were determined to pursue their goals. Profession would not be a significant factor. It would be far more important for these to be the sort of people who earnestly desire and who fully intend to change their entire lives!

Imagine such a dynamic group in one room. Imagine the scintillating discussion on "how we all intend to free ourselves from negativism" and "how we intend to find real answers and a genuine purpose for our lives."

Turning to each person individually, we would first have them make some positive affirmations: "I intend to be a doctor." "I am going to be a writer." "I plan to start a printing business of my own."

Once these affirmations had been made, the group as a whole would attempt to assist each person in formulating a plan for success. A *specific* plan consisting of logical and practical steps. Often it is easier for us to see how another might overcome an obstacle than it is for us to overcome an obstacle of our own. For this reason, we could expect to receive a lot of good advice from people who might be in a better position to help us than WE are. Remember, it is not only through self-knowledge but also through our receptivity to new ideas that we continue to learn and grow!

At the end of the evening, there might be a question-and-answer period, and also, some general discussion. You can be sure it would be a party that would send you home with something more than the promise of a hangover. And the food would not be fattening since it would only be food for thought. ONLY!

From firsthand experience, I can tell you that there is nothing more enjoyable and exhilarating than meeting with others who are capable of stimulating your mind! Stimulating and challenging it in new and exciting ways.

"What if..."
"Have you ever thought about..."
*"If you really want to be daring, why not
try...?"*

That is the way you can expect a lot of sentences to
begin. And isn't that better than:

"Well, I don't know..."
"If I were you, I'd sleep on it...."
"Your chances are one in a million...."

Let me warn you about something. If you present your
ideas to negative people, they will be more than happy
to give you all the "reasons" why your ideas won't work.
The problem you face when listening to the advice of
negative people is that their opinions and reasoning will
seem logical and believable. It is not unusual for negative
people to support their faulty reasoning with a set of
faulty statistics.

Unfortunately, we can use statistics to prove any point.
For instance, what if I told you that the state of Nevada
has more boats per capita than any other state in the
nation? "No, that isn't possible!", you would say. "Nevada
is known for its arid deserts and meager rainfall."

However, let's suppose that there were only three people living in the entire state of Nevada, and all three of
them had boats. My original statement would still hold
true. Nevada would have more boats per capita than any
other state in the nation because everyone who lived
there owned a boat!

While this illustration may border on the ridiculous,
I want you to be aware that a faulty argument can be
built around faulty statistics. Rather than listen to negative people who present believable but faulty arguments

as to why it will be difficult if not impossible for you to achieve your goal, it is in your best interest to receive advice from positive people who have already achieved their dreams and desires.

VISUALIZATION ON A MORE PERSONAL LEVEL

If the principles of Creative Mental Imagery are faithfully followed, they are sure to work in *every* area of your life. As I focused on my dreams and began to follow my new plan for success, I not only began to love myself more, but I found I was more open to a truly loving relationship.

While I experienced a great deal of satisfaction in the area of my life's work, I sensed that there was still something missing. I had an abundance of success and happiness, but no one to share it with. I knew that one of the best things about success is sharing it with someone special.

As I have often said, I believe that timing is one of the key elements to every successful situation. The right thing (or person) entering our lives at the *wrong* time invites certain disaster. It is vitally important that we become sensitive to proper timing when we create what we want. This skill, once mastered, will richly reward us the rest of our lives.

The time came when I knew that circumstances were right for a loving, committed relationship, and so, I decided to use the principles I had been teaching and writing about to create my perfect mate. The reason I am sharing this with you is because I have discovered that loving work, when combined with a loving relationship, gives a human being the most dynamic power he or she will ever possess! I did not know this at the time, but I believed it on an intellectual level. Today, I know it to

be a FACT! To demonstrate exactly how it works, I will
share with you the manner in which I created my perfect
loving relationship, using the principles discussed in this
book, and also, in my previous books.

We have already learned that you must know what you
want before you can have it. The more clearly you are
able to focus on your goals, the faster your subconscious
will manifest it for you. Through a kind of trial-and-error
process, I had gradually gained a clear picture of the
woman I could be happiest with, and also, the woman I
could *make* happy. Her image was so clearly imprinted
upon my mind, right down to specific details and qualifications, that I assumed it would take the rest of my life
to find her! Still, I knew how the mind works, and if it is
focused on the end result, the subconscious has no choice
but to produce it.

I remember discussing all this with my friend Ramon.
(You will meet him in another section of this book.) Ramon believes as strongly as I do in our ability to create
what we want, but in this particular instance, he had a
few doubts.

"Bob, I know this stuff works," he said. "It works for
me and it works for you, but I think you are really lim-
iting yourself by being this specific. There is no perfect
woman out there. You can have *most* of what you want,
but you'll have to be willing to compromise in certain
areas if you hope to find a suitable mate." He then pro-
ceeded to give me the statistical probabilities of meeting
such a person based on each qualification I had mentioned.

The qualifications I had listed were as follows:

1. Age: 30 to 35 years old
2. 5 feet 4 inches to 5 feet 7 inches tall
3. Slim build, looks great in jeans!
4. Pretty eyes
5. Good sense of humor

6. Adventurous
7. Nonmaterialistic
8. Some college background
9. Professionally skilled but not involved in an all-consuming career
10. Compatible in terms of religious beliefs
11. Likes country western music and dancing
12. Financially stable
13. Someone who enjoys horses
14. Preferably from a small-town or country background rather than a city
15. Someone who has no knowledge of who "Dr. Anthony" is
16. Someone who will make we weak in the knees the first time I meet her

Nothing like being specific! I used all the techniques that I have worked with and written about to find the ideal relationship. One thing I have found is that once you are clear on what you want, you should communicate it to others. Why? Because once they are aware of your goal, they can help you attract the right people or circumstances into your life. In my case, the answer came through my secretary, Lee.

One day we were discussing personal relationships, and she said: "You know, I've known you for a very long time, and I've seen you go through many situations in your life. I must admit that I've never seen you quite as ready for the right relationship as you appear to be now. For over a year I've had someone in mind for you, but I never mentioned her because I didn't think the time was right. In any case, I think she is perfect for you. I haven't discussed this with her, but I think the two of you should meet. Why don't I arrange dinner for the three of us so that I can introduce you?"

Through the years, I have learned to trust Lee with all of my innermost secrets, with all of my financial affairs and business dealings, and in view of this, I have come to trust her personal judgment and opinions in matters that concern me. Knowing me as well as she does, I felt confident that the evening would not be a disaster. The worst thing that could happen was that she might not be entirely right. In any case, I was willing to give it a try.

As it turned out, Lee's friend Cyndi lived in Tucson, approximately 110 miles away. What the heck! I thought. It'll be something different to do.

As we drove toward Cyndi's town house near a Tucson mountain preserve, I could feel my anxiety beginning to build. Cyndi had been described to me as an attractive woman, although not a fashion-model type. I began to wonder if Lee was preparing me for a plain-looking woman with the proverbial "great personality."

When we arrived, Cyndi was standing in front of her town house with her dog Bruto on a leash. As we pulled into the drive, I realized I was looking at the loveliest woman I had ever seen. She was slim and tanned, and had a warm and generous smile. As I got out of the car and introduced myself, I realized that I was indeed a bit *weak in the knees*. The feeling appeared to be mutual, for I sensed Cyndi's reaction to me, which she later described as a kind of "electrical shock" as the two of us shook hands.

To make a long story short, she met every qualification I had listed—no exceptions, no compromises. The best way I can describe it is to say that it did not seem like we were meeting for the first time, but more as if we had already known one another a very long time and were just being reunited. Cyndi later confessed to me that only one month before we met, a friend had asked her what kind of man she felt she could become seriously interested in. Rather kiddingly, she responded: "A cowboy or a doctor." In my case, she got both. Remember, your subconscious mind doesn't kid around!

When I related this experience to my friend Ramon, he said: "Okay, Bob, in this case I was very definitely wrong. And believe me, I couldn't be happier!"

Moral of the Story: Don't ever believe that you can't have it all. You CAN! But only if you are willing to TURN ON YOUR DREAM MACHINE!

CHAPTER 6
Winners and Losers

This chapter is about winning. Winning is an attitude. Winners do a number of things that losers refuse to do.

Losing is *also* an attitude. Losers generally want something for nothing. They're greedy; they want to win without doing the required work.

Winners are willing to pay the price of success. The *full* price—no discounts up front! Winning is like starting a fire on a cold winter's day. If you want heat, you must first put wood into the fireplace. The winner gathers wood, lights the fire, and receives the heat he seeks. The loser, on the other hand, stands in front of the fireplace and says, "Give me heat first, then I'll give you wood." The loser refuses to pay the price up front, and in the end, he is still cold.

The one characteristic that all losers and failures share is an inability to delay gratification. They want things NOW! They refuse to invest their time, energy, and money in the present in order to realize a future payoff. Yet, this is the way that all of nature works. First, the seed must be planted. Later, you harvest the crop.

GOING FOR THE GOALS

Winners strive for excellence while losers strive to avoid work. Winners have goals and formulate a plan in order to *achieve* their goals.

Goals represent the measure of our possibilities, the gauge of our progress, the test of our fitness for success. The outstanding leaders of every age have been those who set up their own goals and then consistently exceeded them. Within all of us there are wells of thought and dynamos of energy that we may not know we possess until an emergency arises. Then, we are surprised to find that we are able to put forth double or even triple the amount of energy normally expended, which causes us to realize that we have much more to offer than we originally believed.

Losers have no specific goals. Instead, they daydream about winning the lottery or inheriting a fortune.

We choose to be either a winner or a loser. Each of us has a success mechanism and a failure mechanism. If we choose to activate our success mechanism, our failure mechanism automatically goes off. That is why it is so important to start thinking *SUCCESS*. It is essential that you give yourself the green light to move ahead since no mind can embrace a new idea until it rejects the alternative. Quite simply, it is impossible to think success and failure at the same time. Therefore, you should develop and faithfully follow a plan for your own success. Know your objectives. Have a timetable. Select your methods. And prepare to make certain sacrifices.

Winning starts with belief. If you are going to win consistently, you must see yourself as a winner. Your self-image must be that of a winner. Winning is not a matter of good fortune or good luck. It is a mental attitude. The winner does what is necessary in order to guarantee a successful outcome.

THINK OR SINK

A winner thinks for himself. He does not accept other people's opinions as fact until he has validated the information for himself. Incidentally, your job as a winner, and also as a conscientious reader of this book, is to judge for yourself whether the thoughts and ideas contained herein are of any benefit to you. Put them to the test! Compare them to other methods you have used in the past. It is through the process of thinking for yourself that you will begin *doing* for yourself.

Doing is the opposite of procrastination, a term that conjures up different images for each of us. Perhaps you imagine a procrastinator to be a person who lies under a large shade tree reading a book when he should actually be mowing the lawn. That is *one* kind of procrastinator, but there are also many others. They are to be found in every walk of life, in every profession, in every culture and environment. Procrastinators may differ in age, size, and appearance, but they all have certain things in common. As nonachievers they tend to follow the same pattern of avoidance. And it all begins with their determination to get an early start.

NOT DOING TODAY WHAT YOU CAN PUT OFF FOREVER

At the outset, the procrastinator is extremely hopeful. Believing he has learned from past mistakes, he is reasonably confident that he will never again fall into the same old trap. He vows to get an early start and is determined to do his work in a systematic and timely fashion. But when faced with the "right now" of it, he somehow finds it difficult or impossible to begin. Even so, he is determined to get started—eventually. Operating without any kind of plan, the procrastinator soon realizes that *this* time is really no different from all those *other* times. At this stage, he begins to feel anxious and confused.

As time goes on, the procrastinator is inclined to give himself various ultimatums. *"I must start soon!"* is at the heart of everything he is telling himself, but since the deadline is still not at hand, he continues to delude himself into thinking he is a doer and not just a dreamer.

One day, when he is finally forced to accept the possibility that he may *never* get started, he is overpowered by a dreadful sense of foreboding. He becomes mentally paralyzed as a number of highly unpleasant thoughts begin to buzz around in his brain. Among them is the ugly suspicion that there may be something seriously wrong with him. "It's me! There's something wrong with ME!" he begins muttering to himself. At this point, our frustrated procrastinator is quick to convince himself that he is lacking some basic or fundamental quality that other people possess: self-discipline, intelligence, courage—or luck! After all, no one ELSE has these problems! He is now convinced that he is totally alone.

In the final stage of his dilemma, he must face up to the fact that he has only two choices—he can either see things through to the bitter end, or else he can throw in the towel. By this time, the procrastinator's focus is no longer on how well the job can be done, but on whether it can be done at all.

Beyond this point, it is easy enough to predict what will follow. "Never again!" the procrastinator says, vowing to do things differently the next time.

Once you have become caught up in this self-defeating cycle, your failure mechanism is hard at work. Success is no longer a possibility, unless you begin to realize what success really is. Success is a voyage to a planned destination. It is not a matter of being in the right place at the right time. It is not a matter of good luck. Success happens when opportunity meets preparation, and opportunity is always at hand for the winner.

CONSISTENT PROGRESS—THE TRUE MEASURE OF SUCCESS

Most people confuse achievement with success. The reason for this is that they tend to forget that success is a journey, not a destination. Whatever you consider to be a worthy goal or ideal is what defines success for you. Once you understand the principles of success, you can rise to any level of achievement you choose. But the first thing you must do is to make the *decision* to be successful.

Part of learning to be a success is avoiding the influence of failure. We are all familiar with the old saying: Misery loves company. Unfortunately, it is much worse than that! Misery absolutely *requires* company. A loser feels good about himself when he surrounds himself with other losers. Successful people, on the other hand, have the opposite view. They believe in success. In yours. In theirs. In everybody's! There is something so inspiring, so downright contagious about their attitude.

Henry Ford was a simple entrepreneur, a tinkerer, when he first became friends with Thomas Edison. The example that Edison provided through his attitudes and work habits caused Henry Ford to formulate plans and goals for his inventions. The man Ford had chosen as his friend was one who would later encourage, inspire, and assist him in attaining his goals.

In choosing your own friends and associates, bear in mind that when you spend your time with people who are negative, your attitudes, and ultimately your successes, will suffer. But when you surround yourself with achievers, you will never have to face difficulties alone. You can always ask for, expect, and receive encouragement and support. And you will always have someone who will be ready to celebrate your victories rather than rain on your parade.

WHAT YOU CAN PERCEIVE YOU CAN ACHIEVE

How good are you at *envisioning* success? I strongly urge you never to place any restrictions upon your imagination or desires. As long as you do not restrain them, they will never restrain you.

A reporter once asked Conrad Hilton if he intended to help others be successful now that he had become a success himself. Hilton immediately took issue with the manner in which the question was worded. "Nonsense!" he said. "I was a success when I worked as a clerk in a rooming house. I knew then that I would build a chain of hotels."

The real starting point is desire. The more you want to be a winner, the greater your chance of becoming one. Thoughts have power! At every stage in your life, what you have or *don't* have can be directly attributed to the pattern of your thinking.

It is useless to say that you never get what you want

because you ALWAYS do. Just as a lion receives the experiences of a lion, simply because it IS a lion, so you receive the experiences of the person you are. If you do not particularly care for that person, if you see a real need for change, then it is up to you to alter your thought patterns so that you will begin to receive the experiences of the person you have always wanted to be.

If you use your imagination, you can possess whatever you want at this very moment. Just think of that! You have but to visualize it, to believe in it, in order to bring it into being. If this sounds too good to be true, you might wish to check another source, a much higher source—the Holy Bible. Mark 11:24 tells us: *Therefore I say unto you, What things soever ye desire, when ye pray, believe that ye receive them, and ye shall have them.* This powerful scripture is one of the most often quoted. Why do you suppose this is true? Could it possibly have anything to do with the incredible feeling the passage gives you regarding your own potential? Of course it does! We have God-given talents that constantly seek expression. We have a mission in life that we are yearning to fulfill. This inner quality, this inherent purpose is deeply touched whenever we read MARK 11:24. And that is as it should be!

Always, there is something inside you urging you on, giving you no rest, no peace, no opportunity to abandon your dreams. Occasionally you may be tempted. During periods of despondency or self-doubt, it may seem best to give up. Yet you never quite do. Time and time again, you come back to that deeply buried dream, that small inner voice that continues to prod you onward.

The good news is that the instant you really *want* success, it starts coming into your life. The more you think about success, the more you create it. If you concentrate on things that can keep you from your desires, you actually create your own obstacles. In each case, you set forces into motion that shape and guide your destiny. Great achievement is the result of great thoughts. Poverty is the result of poor thoughts. The choice is yours. You are not a victim. You are a creator.

You have been given the power to accomplish anything you desire. It lies in your imagination, in your dreams. These are the most precious gifts bestowed upon you. If you choose to squander these gifts by listening to those who do not share your dreams, then your dreams are lost. If, on the other hand, you surround yourself with positive thinkers and trust your own talents and instincts, you are on your way to *achieving* your dreams.

A person with a failure mentality believes that there is only so much success to go around, that it is somehow rationed. But the truth is, success is like love. The more you have, the more you have to give. The more you give, the more you *have* to give, and the more you get to keep. Winners know this and act accordingly!

The most significant discovery of the human-potential movement is that you can change your beliefs through your actions as readily as you can change your actions through your beliefs. Your beliefs are what *guide* your actions. It is almost impossible to act in opposition to your beliefs. If you believe that you are a loser, then you are a loser. It is not until you begin to rise above your faulty beliefs that you can hope for a brighter day. If you cannot accept the idea that you are a winner, your *subconscious* will find a way for you to lose.

How does a winner activate his success mechanism? The answer is simple. First, you must make a commitment to the thing you wish to accomplish. Second, you should learn all you can from *experts*. Experts are people who are successfully doing what you want to do. Experts are also people who enjoy sharing what they know with those who are genuine seekers.

Have you ever considered taking a successful person

to lunch? Can you think of a better way, a less expensive way, to avail yourself of that person's professional expertise? Consulting fees normally range from one hundred to five hundred dollars per hour. Are you beginning to see the rationale here? Although a loser might argue that a wealthy person can well afford to pick up his own tab, I say this is one of the best investments you can possibly make. I have rarely met a successful person who wasn't happy to share his or her ideas with a potential winner. In fact, successful people take great pride in helping others. You've undoubtedly heard the saying: "The bigger they are, the nicer they are." Well, it's really true!

Lao-tzu once said: "A journey of a thousand miles begins with a single step." The winner takes that step. Winners have the ability to focus on a larger goal, which they generally accomplish through a series of smaller goals. Success is the journey. Achievement is the realization of the goal.

MAKING THE IMPOSSIBLE POSSIBLE

Once the horseless carriage had been invented, other minds went to work on that basic concept and quickly developed it to its present state of mechanical maturity. Things start to work once human endeavor has been accelerated by one person's superior vision and refusal to contemplate failure.

Unconsciously, we tend to classify things as either possible or impossible. Winners are those who dare to tackle the impossible, and who KEEP tackling it again and again.

The more you surrender to inhibition, the more greedy inhibition becomes. Before very long, you will be unwilling to attempt anything that involves an element of risk. But if you try to accomplish the thing that is beyond you, you will increase your powers *just that much*. Think about that! If you clearly visualize your plans and dreams, you can be sure that your talents, time, and desires will come to your aid. If you use them fully, with confidence and determination, you are destined to achieve your goals.

Have you ever stopped to consider the actual situation whenever you insist to yourself that you WILL do something, no matter how difficult or seemingly impossible a task it might be? Perhaps it hadn't occurred to you that there really is a WILL involved.

The human will is an active, living force. In making an analysis of the attributes of successful people, it soon becomes apparent that the one prevailing characteristic seems to be an indomitable will. It is unfortunate that this term has acquired a somewhat negative connotation, particularly in the way it is used to describe a strong-willed individual. If you have ever heard a parent refer to a child as "exceptionally strong-willed," you were undoubtedly listening to someone complain about a child's propensity to demand his or her own way. And while there can certainly be some problems connected with this kind of behavior, it is important to realize that there is also a mature way of exercising one's will. To know rightly is to think rightly, and to think rightly is to will rightly. Once we clearly understand this, it is doubtful that we will ever try to exercise our will in a cruel or selfish way. What we are really talking about here is the *energy of determination*. Without this energy, you will accomplish very little in life.

According to an ancient Chinese proverb: Great souls have wills; feeble ones have only wishes. How very true!

We can argue or debate the matter forever, but the facts remain the same. Strong-willed people dare to do what others will not. They endeavor to accomplish what others will not even attempt. In short, they make the impossible possible!

When he was at the height of his career as America's most famous magazine editor, George Horace Lorimer wrote a brief editorial for his *Saturday Evening Post* entitled "The Fairy Wand." It read as follows:

> Most young men of ambition are in constant search of those who will help them on the road to success. Such aid is found in many ways and through many persons. It may come through friends, chance acquaintances, books, and formal education. It may take the form of wise advice, searching criticism, and disinterested appraisal of character. It may be free or bought and paid for. It may be amateur or professional. It may be found in the lives of great men, in casual anecdote, in textbook theory, in everyday experience, or in the observation of one's associates.
>
> But no outsider, no outside force can wave the wand that brings success. Fundamentally, it is not to be found in other persons, in books or lectures or even in observation. Deeds and not words are what put men on top. The successful man may gain help and inspiration from others ... but he always blazes a trail of his own.

A LIFE OF QUALITY

At this very moment, you are either seriously or casually committed to the idea of success. If you are totally committed and able to understand and consistently move in the direction of your personal goals, you are on your way to becoming a winner.

Your future is up to you. Stop looking back. Look ahead. Assume total responsibility for where you are today and where you are going.

Be willing to:

1. Take positive action
2. Work hard
3. Define your objectives
4. Give more than you take
5. Learn from adversity
6. Become involved
7. Remain true to your goals
8. Remain optimistic
9. Be confident and enthusiastic
10. Persist! Persist! Persist!

Fix your mind firmly upon anything at all—good or bad—and you will invariably attract it. Sweep from the chambers of your mind all miserable, negative thoughts like: I can't. That's just my luck. Poor me.

Begin at this very moment to create a new ideal—an image of personal and financial success. Allow yourself to SEE it mentally. Except it! Demand it! In so doing, you will be creating an entirely new mental attitude. You *have* that ability. USE it! Make every thought that comes into your mind work for you. The quality of your thought is the measure of your power. Think of the value of effort, not just success. You can't always win, and you'll never be perfect. But you can keep on trying and always do your best. Think of your performance, not of yourself. Never confuse what you do with what you are, or what you're worth. You'll undoubtedly make mistakes, but you'll also learn from them and become a better person for it.

SALVAGING SCRAP TIME

Scrap time is any time that would normally be wasted. It includes periods of waiting, driving, walking, or jogging—or any time that you are occupied with a task that takes virtually no thought, i.e.: opening mail, organizing files, performing mundane chores. During such times, you may wish to daydream or listen to the radio, but you could also be doing something more meaningful, something that will assist you in achieving your long-range goals.

1. *Listen to an informative tape.* There are many excellent audio-cassette programs available to help you motivate yourself. These are particularly good to listen to first thing in the morning, perhaps while you are getting dressed, or late at night, just before you go to bed. Some part of every day should be devoted to motivating yourself in a really positive way. Audio-cassette tapes provide you with an excellent means of doing this!

2. *Read.* While waiting, read books or magazines that will provide you with useful information. If you hate waiting in line or being put on hold after placing a call, you don't need to just wait. You could also be *doing* something, even *learning* something, and in the process, pass the time more quickly.

3. *Review or critique your day in terms of how effectively your time was spent.* This is a little mental exercise you can perform any time your mind is not otherwise occupied. It is good to reflect upon your daily progress in order to determine exactly how well you are doing.

4. *Plan ahead.* Success is never an accident. It takes thoughtful planning. Plan for tomorrow, for the

month, or even for the year. First, work out your strategy for success, then *go out and give it all you've got!*

(NOTE: Once you have learned how to salvage scrap time, you will discover "hidden" hours in the day. Scraps of time add up quickly. Just ten minutes per day is equal to one workweek per year.)

Winners don't waste idle moments! They know their time is valuable. For those earning $50,000 per year, twenty minutes of each working day is worth $2,043 annually. How would *you* feel about throwing away two thousand dollars each year? How you use your time represents a deliberate choice. I urge you to choose wisely and well!

THE WINNING APPROACH

In life, you can move forward, move backward, or stand still. Through self-analysis, you can easily determine in which direction you are going.

When you ask yourself important questions such as those that follow, be sure to give honest answers. Remember that nothing is ever accomplished through self-deception—only through self-analysis.

1. Have I attained the goals I established for myself this week/month/year?   Yes _____   No _____
2. Has the spirit of my conduct and overall attitude been positive in nature? Yes _____   No _____
3. Have I allowed the habit of procrastination to decrease my efficiency?   Yes _____   No _____
4. Have I been persistent in seeing my plans through to completion?   Yes _____   No _____

5. Have I diligently budgeted my time?
                          Yes _____ No _____
6. Have I allowed any negative thoughts to influence
   me?   Yes _____ No _____

Remember, inventing excuses to explain away failure is the loser's way! Don't waste any time or energy on excuses. Starting today—be a WINNER!

CHAPTER 7
Risk and Other Four-Letter Words

There are three basic personality types that are doomed to a life of failure: victims, sustainers, and dreamers.

VICTIMS are people who focus on the past and who concern themselves with how things "should have been." Victims feel helpless and spend much of their time blaming others for what has happened to them. They view themselves as pawns in the game of life, believing they have no control over their past, present, or future. They feel they are always in the wrong place at the wrong time. Usually, they are preoccupied with problems that are totally out of their control—problems such as what is going to happen to the economy or whether or not it is apt to rain tomorrow.

Victims often associate with other victims and feel they are persecuted as a group. This helps to reinforce their belief that they are absolutely right in their thinking. They often blame their parents or family for what has happened to them (or not happened to them). They believe that they will continue to have rotten luck and that nothing can be done about it. In any case, it isn't THEIR fault!

SUSTAINERS, on the other hand, are people who are so focused on their present condition that they stay right where they are. Sustainers go through life as if they were running in place. Sustainers resist change. Their primary goals are safety and security. They seldom plan for the future, and spend most of their time fighting anything that threatens to change their immediate situation. Their major objective is to maintain the *status quo*. In other words, they are not inclined to rock the boat.

DREAMERS are people who plan for the future but never turn their plans into action. They prefer to live within the safety of their ideas, without taking the risks that are necessary to make things happen. As time goes on, they tend to become increasingly unhappy and disillusioned because their lives never seem to match up with their dreams.

All of these people have one thing in common: they are trapped in their present circumstances and see no way out. They are defeated by their unwillingness to RISK. Whenever an individual forgoes risk, he has generally convinced himself that he is living cautiously and that it is "better to be safe than sorry."

IS it?

As we attempt to address this issue, you are urged to decide for yourself if anything worth having is ever possible without some element of risk—if life is even worth *living* without it.

ARE YOU A TAKER OR A MAKER?

Takers are people who feel there is never enough to go around, so the only way to have anything at all is to take it from others. They also believe in luck. But they seldom believe in risk.

Makers are people who know that if it's ever going to

happen, it's up to them! They MAKE things happen by believing in themselves, by forging ahead, and also, by daring to risk.

THE SECURITY TRAP

Security is an interesting concept or theory. There is really no other way to look at it since security does not even exist. If you talk to anyone who has lived through a war, the Great Depression, or even a major hurricane or earthquake, you will learn how quickly every form of comfort and security can be torn away.

Living is a risky business! Being born involves a certain amount of risk. Driving a car or becoming ill is also risky. In the course of a single day, you will take any number of risks, although you may not always be aware of them. The next time you cross a street, you might give this some thought.

Where is it written that every vehicle on the road will automatically stop when the light turns red, enabling you to cross safely? As we all know, and as accident statistics continue to inform us, some cars run red lights. And yet we trust that everything will work out as planned. Whenever you cross the street, you assume the risk of getting to the other side. You feel reasonably secure that you will make it. But why should you, when all forms of security are an illusion? No matter how secure you think you are, there is always some way in which you can lose. Does this mean you should never cross the street? No, of course not. Nor should you allow yourself to become unduly concerned with the idea of losing, because if you do, you will only be working against yourself.

You will lose whatever you are afraid to lose. Whenever you become unduly concerned with loss, you automatically *set yourself up* to lose. Nothing in your life will be secure until you become secure within.

The only true security is the ability to actualize—*to make real through action*. Once we have mastered the ability to actualize, we know that no matter where we are, no matter what the economic conditions, we can create what we want—as long as we truly WANT it. This is true security!

The biggest risk in life is in NOT risking. If you don't take risks, you will never have what you want. The fact is, all desires come with some form of risk. *NO RISK— NO REWARD!*

WHAT ARE YOU AFRAID OF?

It is impossible to discuss risk without also discussing fear, since the two are so closely related. If we do not take risks, it is because we are afraid. And yet, legitimate fears have a purpose in our lives. Taking this into account, would you be inclined to say that fear is your enemy or your friend?

Let's imagine the following scenario:

One night, while you are walking along a lonely mountain road, a huge lion suddenly leaps out into your path. As he prepares to attack, you are overwhelmed with fear, and your only thought is to survive in whatever way you can.

Fear, in this instance, is your friend. It will immediately trigger those physical responses that make it possible for you to run faster than you have ever run before. A sudden powerful surge of adrenaline will come pouring into your bloodstream, and due to faster breathing, a greater oxygen supply to the muscles will enable you to do whatever you can, whatever you *must*, in order to escape with your life.

In this particular situation, it is not necessary for you to think about being afraid. Fear is an automatic and appropriate response to any life-threatening situation. The human brain and nervous system are designed to react to the problems and challenges of everyday life— but circumstances are not always what they seem.

What if the lion is not really a lion at all? What if it is actually a practical joker outfitted in a lion costume, someone you know who thought it might be fun to give you a good scare? Why should you be afraid of a person in a lion's costume? Ah, but you didn't KNOW it was a costume, at least not at first. And during those moments, your brain and nervous system reacted not to what was there, but to what you *believed* was there. And so it is with so many of our unfounded fears. Each day, we go along, fearful of the way we perceive things to be when, in fact, our perceptions are entirely wrong.

Why do you suppose, whenever risk is involved, most of us tend to think only in terms of loss? After all, there is also a winning side to consider here. It is the other option—the other potential outcome—and yet it is never quite as real to us as the possibility of loss.

The fact is, we have conditioned ourselves to experience this fear. It is not based on anything that actually exists, only on what we imagine to be true. So many of our fears are not "real lions" at all, but they are enough to keep us afraid.

If you were to ask other people what they are most afraid of, many would be unable to tell you. As you listened to their vague answers, it would soon become apparent that what most people actually fear is the unknown.

EXPLORING THE UNKNOWN

A few years ago, a friend of mine asked me to interpret a dream. To her the dream seemed like a senseless jumble of events; I thought it contained an extraordinary message!

In the dream, my friend was awakened by a loud commotion. Running to the window, she saw that her favorite horse was being attacked in the corral by a "huge black blob." The blob was impossible to distinguish—impossible to identify as a bear, a lion, or anything at all.

Reaching into the drawer of her nightstand, my friend grabbed a gun and ran outside, determined to save her horse from this mysterious but ominous threat. She stood anxiously by, waiting for just the right moment, then raised her gun and fired.

"What happened then?" I asked, whereupon my friend responded with a kind of sheepish grin.

"I'm glad it was only a dream," she said, "for when I went to pull the trigger, I discovered that it wasn't even a gun that I was holding. It was a flashlight!"

"That's very interesting," I said. "Very interesting indeed!"

"Why is it interesting?" my friend immediately asked. "It's absurd! To begin with, I don't even own a horse. And secondly, to be caught with a flashlight at a time when you really need a gun seems like the height of stupidity to me."

"Well, that's one way of looking at it," I told her. "But there's also another way. The dream is highly symbolic in the sense that the black blob you saw represents anything 'unknown' to you. As you've already said, it was impossible to distinguish what it was that was threatening your horse. Running out into the night, you were determined to confront the unknown, but not the way so many other people might have. Rather than attempting to attack or destroy it, you were more interested in shedding some light on it."

At that, my friend sat back and seriously considered this interpretation of her dream. "I suppose that could be true," she said, and based on what I already knew about her, I was inclined to agree.

This was a person who possessed a basically inquisitive nature, someone who had always welcomed the challenge to learn more about whatever it was she did not understand. I had never known her to feel intimidated or threatened by the unknown. On the contrary, she had always been intrigued by it.

What about you? While I would never attempt to suggest that you should live without fear, since we already know that certain forms of fear are necessary to our survival, still, I believe it is important to put our fears in the proper perspective.

Every new environment, every new experience in life will cause you a few anxious moments. Anything unfamiliar or "unknown" may well encourage some feelings of timidity or fear. But there is something you can do about those feelings. There are ways of analyzing them, overcoming them, and/or using them to your advantage.

The first thing you should do whenever you encounter a so-called fearful situation is analyze your response. Is it an automatic response, one you quickly revert to simply out of habit? Over a period of time, has it gradually become as familiar to you as a comfortable old shoe?

YOUR BEHAVIOR WILL MATCH YOUR PICTURE OF YOURSELF

"I know I shouldn't react this way, but I just can't help it! That's just the way I am!"

How often have you heard someone say that? How often have *you* said it? What are you really saying when you say this? You are admitting that you are locked into an automatic response—that there is nothing you can do to change it. You are stuck with it!

Let us assume for the moment that job interviews have always made you exceedingly nervous and that you have an interview coming up tomorrow. Based upon your past experiences, you know that you will find it difficult to cool your heels in someone's outer office, and by the time you are called in, you will undoubtedly be a nervous wreck. Why? Because that's the way it has always been.

But why do things have to be the way they have always been? Humans, unlike members of the animal kingdom, have the ability to control their emotions. They need never be controlled by their automatic responses, except in situations involving dire emergencies. One way to alter your response is to concentrate on the *positive* rather than the *negative* side of the ledger.

Fact: You are waiting to be interviewed for a job you are obviously capable of performing or you would not have answered the ad. Through the years, you have acquired a great deal of experience in and knowledge of your particular field. You are undoubtedly more capable than many others who have been interviewed thus far, and you are both eager and willing to do a good job. You *want* this job. You *need* this job. You are qualified to do it. So, why wouldn't a potential employer seriously consider your application?

Based on my own experiences as a potential employer, I can tell you that people I did not hire were rarely turned away because they lacked professional skills. More often than not, it was some negative quality they communicated to me that made me decide against hiring them. Perhaps they did not speak with enough confidence and authority, or did not demonstrate an adequate amount of pride in themselves and their capabilities. Those who presented themselves in the *right* way have never had a problem convincing me that they were right for the job. In some cases, it was even possible for me to make my decision over the phone, before I even met them personally. Does this mean I am an impulsive decision maker? There are those who might think so, but my track record speaks for itself. Through the years, I have rarely misjudged people and have invariably employed those who were the most capable of doing the job. The people I hired never exhibited any unsettling fears, even in cases where they were forced to admit that their knowledge or experience fell a little short of what I was looking for. Sensing that they were willing to learn, I was willing to teach them.

YOU CAN NEVER FAIL!

Fail. This is the third and last in a series of four-letter words which need to be discussed in conjunction with *risk* and *fear.*

Why is it that we fear risk? Because we might fail. Do you think you will NOT fail if you choose to do nothing at all? If so, then you and I have a totally different concept of failure. To begin with, it is important to understand that you can never fail as a person. Your job may fail, or your business, or some personal relationship in which you are involved. Those things can fail, but you cannot fail. You should never identify with your failures, because if you do, you will immediately lose sight of this very important fact: *any situation in which you are involved can be changed in some way so that it ultimately becomes a successful learning experience.* You can actually PROFIT from failure. And you should. Always!

There are also ways to *avoid* failure, and you should remember them as you work toward your goals. To begin with, remember that success is a process, not something you achieve all at once. It is wrong to give yourself Herculean tasks to perform and unrealistic time frames in which to perform them. If you have never earned any great amount of money, it is doubtful that you will earn a million dollars in the next few months. Nor should that be your goal. Your goal should be to improve upon your past performance record because constant, steady progress will eventually lead you to the million dollars you seek.

If you were to talk with Olympic-gold-medal winners, they would tell you that they did not begin their winning careers by jumping the highest hurdles, by lifting the heaviest weights, or by running the longest distances. Instead, they challenged themselves a little more, and then a little more, until they finally became the world champions they are today. Along the way, you may be sure they enjoyed each goal that they achieved. Bronze- or silver-medal winners do not crucify themselves over not having gained the gold. Rather, they think of what it has taken to become a bronze- or silver-medal winner, of all the contestants in all the world who had to be eliminated, people they successfully outperformed in order to gain this fine award. To even *compete* in the Olympics, whether any prize is won or not, is an achievement in itself. True athletes know this. They know it because they are true winners, constantly striving to improve, to grow, to be better than the day before. They are success oriented, not failure oriented.

A MATTER OF DISCIPLINE

Another way to avoid failure is to practice self-discipline. As a successful author, I am frequently approached by others who enjoy writing and who would like to make writing their chosen career. They see it as an exciting, even glamorous way of life and ask the sort of questions that invite some reinforcement of that image. Unfortunately, I am rarely able to tell them what they would like to hear. On the other hand, I have no problem with telling them what is actually required. As I review some of these points, you might wish to consider how these methods could also be applied to other areas of expertise. I think you will see that regardless of your job or profession, a little self-discipline can increase your chances for success.

- It is important to select and maintain certain working hours, preferably those that suit you best. It doesn't matter what hours you choose, only that you faithfully adhere to the schedule you have established for yourself.
- Never allow yourself to become discouraged when the words "just don't come," when the typewriter or word processor breaks down, when you just don't feel like writing. Write anyway! You may end up throwing most of it away, but more often than not, you will find that the effort to write removes writer's block. If nothing else, you will write all the garbage out of your system. Then again, you may

find that the part of your work that comes the hardest is also the BEST."

- Force yourself to cut and polish. For a while, it may seem tedious, but pride in your work will eventually take over, and soon, editing and revising will become second nature.

- Try to avoid interruptions—anything that will take you away from your work. This is not the time to sort through your mail, to let neighbors engage you in conversation, or to take out the trash. A luncheon date is almost certain to impede your creative flow, and the prospect of a dinner engagement will be an even greater distraction.

- Don't allow others to lure you away from your work by branding you "antisocial." If you had no interest in people, you wouldn't spend so much of your time writing about them. Don't feel compelled to give excuses or apologies to others. If your friends don't understand what your work requires of you, perhaps they aren't really your friends.

- Be sure you achieve your daily quota—a specific number of words or pages to be written each day. *No matter what!*

These requirements may make writing seem like a tedious job, especially to those who had hoped that they could somehow escape the "everydayness" of it, that as creatively inspired souls, they would have greater freedoms in this world, that dogged determination and discipline would not have a part in things. Sorry! If you are a writer (unpublished) who would like to be an author (published), there are certain things you simply MUST do!

Reread the self-disciplinary methods outlined above and see how many can be successfully applied to your field of endeavor. Don't try to fool yourself into thinking there are any shortcuts, for there aren't. Why should there be? Why should you even WANT there to be? You are a doer, a winner, a success-oriented person. You cannot allow yourself to become immobilized by a fear of failure. If you do, you will become another kind of person.

A HORROR-SCOPE APPROACH TO LIFE

Do you believe that failure is written in the stars? Do you think that things are "fated" to happen a certain way? What things? Why?

If you allow yourself to become immobilized by such fatalistic thoughts, you will stop asking yourself such questions, or any questions at all. You will lose the ability to think independently, to take charge of your life, to do anything other than to wait for the world to come crashing down around your ears.

This gloom-and-doom approach to life is totally unrealistic. It has no basis in fact; it is simply an *attitude*. Attitudes obscure facts. Your attitudes can cause you to exaggerate the nature of your difficulties.

The best way to resolve any problem is to put aside your attitudes and exercise your logic. Attack the problem in logical stages. First you do one thing, then another, and then another. Speak to any recovered alcoholic and you will see exactly what I mean. This is a person who does not attempt to effect a permanent cure to his problem, one that will see him through the rest of his life. No, he wants to get through today. And then tomorrow. And then the next day.

This is the most realistic approach to any problem. You can only take care of today. Tomorrow you can take it a step farther. And so on. In this way, you can deal with your difficulty without becoming totally overwhelmed by it. The problem will remain outside you. It will never BECOME you. Here is an important thing to remember! The manner in which you deal with a problem will ultimately determine how it is resolved.

Consider a situation in which you are concerned with an overdue car payment.

Approach #1: If I don't make my car payment soon, my car will be repossessed!

Approach #2: There is a matter concerning an upcoming bill that needs to be resolved in the most practical and expeditious manner.

Approach #1 is enough to throw you into a panic! "Oh my God! What am I going to do?" is the immediate and altogether useless reaction. What such a person usually ends up doing is nothing at all. He continues to fret and stew until the thing he has been worrying about eventually comes to pass.

Approach #2 places the problem at a distance. In other words, there is the problem and there is also you. You are NOT the problem, but rather the person who will eventually OVERCOME the problem. It is important to see yourself in this light, to know you have the capability to resolve your difficulties, and to remind yourself that you have successfully exercised it many times in the past. How did you get this far in life? Was everything coincidence and luck? No. You may be sure you had a hand in things. Given a certain set of circumstances, you objectively evaluated them, then after considering various options, decided upon a specific plan of action. This is how problems are solved. Panic and hysteria have no part in problem solving.

Continue to remind yourself that you are always free to accept or reject your fear of failure. Moreoever, you are always in a position to use it for your own benefit.

ACCENTUATING THE POSITIVE

The best way to dispel any negative thoughts or feelings is to chase them away with positive ones. Don't try to fight down your fears or anxieties. Replace them with something else!

During times of stress, have you ever had a sudden urge to escape the environment that has become so unpleasant to you? Perhaps you went up to the mountains or went down to the seashore and just sat on a rock and stared out across the water. When you did this, what happened? Were your problems solved? No, but your negative thoughts were dispelled by positive ones. Once you allowed yourself to calm down, you began to see things in their proper perspective. You began to consider some aspects of your situation you had not considered before. You began to see some potential solutions, and soon, you found yourself immersed in some new and exciting ideas. Through it all, the only thing that really changed was your *attitude*. But that was enough. It was enough to give you back a little of that "winning feeling," and soon you were back in the race, running as hard and fast as ever.

Risk. Fear. Fail. Remember these words and do not permit yourself to identify with them! These are the mental states of those who have not yet chosen to replace them with *Challenge, Confidence, and Success*.

If you are presently unhappy with your life, remember, you have the ability to change it! Begin by seeing RISK as CHALLENGE, by overpowering FEAR with CONFIDENCE, and turning FAILURE into SUCCESS. You can do it, just as you have already done so many other things in your life.

If it is security you want, then you need to understand that your security lies in your ability to handle any situation as it happens. That is the only form of security that exists. Everything else can be taken away from you. And since everything else CAN be taken away from you, what is really at risk? Nothing. Whatever is lost is something you can regain, in the same way you achieved it in the first place.

In the final analysis, you are the answer.

Your only real bank account is YOU!

CHAPTER 8
Achieving Wealth and Financial Freedom

Exactly what is money and what does it mean to you?

Although you may believe you have already given this question some serious thought, I would like to challenge your present idea of money by suggesting that it means something quite different to you than you think. The fact is, people do not really like money—*only what money can buy*.

Money is a means to an end. There would be no purpose in earning money, in saving it, or even stockpiling it under your bed if it had no buying power. So, what you really like when you say you like money is what money can buy.

A METHOD OF KEEPING SCORE

In the lives of many, money serves yet another function. Consider the wealthiest wheeler-dealers in the world, those who continue to involve themselves in major acquisitions, who work *hard* at making money, even though they already have all they will ever need. For them, money is a measure of success, a method of keeping score.

Perhaps your own feeling about money is a combination of the two definitions above. If so, you see money in its proper context, and now, it is simply a matter of earning as much as you feel you need.

What is the best way to earn money?

You should never underestimate the importance of this question, for the answer is almost certain to direct the course of your entire life.

Let us assume you believe that the best way to earn money is through any means available to you. While this course of thinking could easily lead you into any number of illegal and potentially hazardous activities, it could also lead you into a life of dead-end jobs. And while you may feel that earning a lot of money is an end in itself, you will eventually realize that something is missing, that you are not entirely happy or fulfilled by your career choice.

Each of us has natural talents and abilities, and one of the most gratifying ways to use them is in your life's work. This method also enables you to look upon work as a pleasurable experience, something to be anticipated, something to jump out of bed and eagerly prepare yourselves for each and every day.

How sad it is that most of us think of our jobs or careers merely as a means of survival. You were not born just to survive!

STUDYING THE WINNERS

When you take the time to study people who are truly successful, you'll see that these people love what they do, that they are doing their "right work." Did you think they chose their professions only because they were lucrative? Think again! How well do you suppose they would do at something they hated the very idea of, something that made them feel chained to their desks, something limited in terms of advancement opportunities? Successful people enjoy their work! They enjoy it because they are good at it and because it is the right thing for them to be doing. In many cases, successful people will even admit that their work was once their hobby.

DOING WHAT YOU LOVE
PAYS OFF!

Doing what you love and loving what you do will automatically ensure your future financial security.

There is no way you can be assured of having more money just because you are willing to change jobs or careers. Rather, financial success lies in what you ultimately decide to do.

TAKING CHARGE OF
WHAT TO CHARGE

If you want to turn the activities you love into a career, you must begin to charge for the services you perform. When you charge for doing something you love to do, you deliver the positive message to your subconscious mind that your time, energy, and skills are indeed valuable.

Too many people only accept money for doing jobs they do not like. The message they deliver to their subconscious mind is that it is not possible to make a living doing what you love to do.

Although you may not feel entirely justified in charging for services rendered while you are still learning a new skill or trade, you should do so as quickly as possible, even if the fee charged is relatively small. It is important to begin associating what you love to do with earning money.

Your beliefs about money inevitably determine how you attract it, spend it, and relate to it. Do you sincerely believe it is possible to make money doing what you love to do? Or do you believe that making money requires doing something you *don't* want to do but which seems essential to your survival?

Here is another important question to ask yourself: Do you sincerely believe that you deserve to be successful or rich? If the answer is no, you should immediately attempt to isolate the reason for this feeling. Don't be surprised if it all goes back to something in your childhood, to a certain amount of negative conditioning from your parents. Once you discover that a certain belief is holding you back, you can make the choice to let go of it and replace it with a new one.

UNLEARNING THE THINGS YOU WERE TAUGHT

How did your parents feel about money? About earning it, saving it, or spending it?

Do you remember being told that you "can't have everything you want"? That you should "save for a rainy day"? That you should "clean your plate because of all the starving kids in China"? That you should "be grateful for what little you have because of others who have nothing at all"?

When you heard these messages, did they seem inspiring to you? Probably not. More than likely, you felt guilty about the resentment you experienced as these messages were repeated over and over again. Why do you suppose you were unable to sympathize with or relate to the messages being conveyed? Because each and every one of them is a *Poverty Message,* and it is only natural to try to avoid poverty consciousness, to want to feel more optimistic and enthusiastic about your future prospects, your life's work.

Poverty Messages do not inspire us to "go for the gold," to pursue any specific career with great enthusiasm or determination. Rather, Poverty Messages encourage us to eke out a living however we can, to be happy to be employed when other are not, to settle for whatever is available to us.

Your parents should not be blamed. From their immediate level of awareness, they were only advising you in the best way they knew. And, of course, what they told you had also been passed down to them by their well-intentioned parents. And so it goes. But it need go no farther. It can stop with you. Right now! TODAY!

Psychologists far and wide have determined that it is detrimental to a person's health and well-being to exist in conflict, to be divided against himself. When you falsely assume that work is one thing and pleasure is another, you are automatically in conflict. There is the thing you *want* to do and the thing you feel you *must* do. How much better life would be if you could unify these two ideas, make them one, and also, make them your life's work. Yes, it IS possible! It is also vital to your good health and happiness.

If you already know this but are afraid of depriving yourself financially, if you fear you will literally cut your income in two by pursuing your dreams, consider this: the real illusion about money is that it creates security. Security does not come from accumulating wealth. I know many people who are extremely wealthy and are still very insecure. In fact, if you feel insecure right now, having more money will only *increase* your feelings of insecurity, since you will then have even *more* of it to lose.

The solution to this particular anxiety is to create activities and circumstances that would make you happy even if you did not have money. When we believe that money is the key to every kind of human satisfaction, it ceases to be a tool and becomes our master. As we acquire more money, we have a tendency to acquire more material possessions. But these possessions can *also* become our master because they will require some form of care and maintenance, or will need to be repaired, protected, or moved about. In other words, whatever you own also owns you!

While there is nothing wrong with wanting to better your life, to have a certain amount of comfort and convenience, you will enjoy these things more if they are not your primary concern, if instead your primary concern is to earn your living by doing something you truly enjoy.

SETTING TANGIBLE GOALS

Assuming you already know what your life's work should be, it then becomes necessary to ask yourself some specific questions about money. How much of it do you need? How much will make you happy?

If you have an earnest desire to be rich, it is not enough to envision yourself earning "a lot of money." How much money is "a lot"? If you expect your subconscious mind to go to work on this desire, you will need to be more specific. And also more practical, in the interests of not allowing yourself to become discouraged early on.

Let us assume you are presently earning minimum wage at some job you do not care to do any longer than necessary. Do you think it would be reasonable to visualize yourself earning a million dollars within the year? Of course not.

The first step is to envision yourself earning *more* than you are presently earning. Your first realistic goal might be to earn an additional one hundred dollars per month. Once you manage to do this, you will experience the euphoric feeling that comes with having reached your first financial milestone. What is really important here, much more important than the extra one hundred dollars per month, is knowing that you can achieve your goals! You need never again wonder whether or not you can do this, for you have just proved to yourself you can! And having proved it, you are now ready to go on, to set a second goal, and to achieve it as well.

There is an important principle at work here that is the very essence of a creative life. A creative life has continuity of purpose. Past achievements are perpetually replaced by future goals. A constant fire of enthusiasm and ambition comprises the fuel of a meaningful existence. No day can dawn without self-direction or motivation. There must be a target and an arrow directed at its center to be replaced daily by another target and yet another arrow.

And so it is with money. For now, it would be best to imagine yourself having a little more. When you start with amounts that you believe are possible, you will have a "success experience" in earning these amounts and thereby reinforce your ability to earn even more.

THE POWER OF BELIEVING

If you want more money, you can cultivate new beliefs that will help you to acquire it. For example, the belief that you can make a living doing what you love to do will motivate you to be creative, and through your creativity, you will make more money than you have ever made before.

Believe it!

But before you can attract more money, you will need to strengthen your resolve and your feelings of entitlement.

Ask yourself right now: Is there any reason why I cannot have this in my life? Do I deserve it? Do I think others are more deserving than I?

It is important to realize that a thing will never materialize for you until you sincerely believe you have earned it. Wanting, in itself, is not enough. Needing something is also not enough. And wishing for it is simply fantasizing.

It is an interesting fact that need is not as strong a motivator as you might have thought. People quite often respond to a want before they will satisfy a need. Why do you suppose this is true?

If we were to ask our parents, they would probably tell us that it is because we have never learned how to manage money, or because we have no sense of responsibility, or because we simply enjoy frivolous spending. But the fact is, there is more to it than that.

Needs require intellectual decisions. A man might come to realize that the roof on his house is leaking and requires some repairs. However, his decision to *do* something about it could be delayed indefinitely. Need in itself, then, is not necessarily a motivating force.

But what about those things we really *want*? A want requires both an intellectual and an emotional decision. And it is the emotion involved that causes us to act.

"I want it so bad I can taste it!"

Haven't we all said that at one time or another? And if the desire was strong enough, whatever we were referring to at the time usually found its way into our lives. Once a high degree of emotion is involved, it is difficult for anyone to dissuade us. We know what we want and we are determined to acquire it.

GOING WITH THE FLOW

As you become more conscious of the thoughts and actions that produce money in your life, you will realize that money flows in and out like ocean tides. You will experience times when the tide is in, and also times when the tide is out. Some months you will have more money than usual, and some months you will have less. Some weeks the volume of business you enjoy may be truly exceptional, and at other times, it may prove to be unusually slow.

Everything in life is cyclical. Just as nature has its cycles, so too is there a natural rhythm or cycle connected with the flow of money. Once you clearly understand this, you will no longer be adversely affected by the "slow times." Whatever the situation is today, you may be sure it is already changing. Gradually. As subtlely as the seasons.

Look at your monthly bank statements and you will soon recognize the ebb and flow of your finances. While we all look forward to the flow, it is necessary to prepare in advance for its reversal. The best way to do this is to keep expenses far enough below your highest income figure that you can handle slow times when they come.

Bear in mind that no matter how well you master the art of earning money, you will always be in trouble if you spend more than you make. What good is a million-dollar income if you are spending a million and one? It is not the amount you earn, but rather the way in which you handle your finances that makes the vital difference.

If you are experiencing an ebb, it is important not to allow yourself to become emotionally off balance. At such times, do not lose confidence in yourself, or begin to equate slow times with failure. Keep reminding yourself that everything in life is cyclical, and that all phases are temporary.

MAKING THE MOST OF THE LEAST

During slow times, it is still possible to be productive and creative. You can begin by analyzing the downturn in an effort to keep it from happening again. Ask yourself how you might have impeded or limited yourself, how you might have done things differently.

If you are a salesperson by profession, is it possible that you have allowed yourself to become too comfortable with the clients you presently serve, and that you have stopped prospecting for more? If so, you need to remind yourself that even customers of long-standing can be lured away, that they can move away, or even pass away. For these reasons and others, a salesperson should always be looking for new prospects to replace those that are lost.

During ebb times, you also have an excellent opportunity to add to your overall knowledge and skill. While things are slow, you can read up on the latest developments in your field, you can attend classes and seminars and make important new contacts. There will also be time to explore new avenues of operation—possible an offshoot of the business in which you are presently engaged. Let those creative juices flow! Some of your ideas could well be worth a fortune.

STOP WORRYING—START CREATING

During ebb times, it is totally useless and counterproductive to fret about paying your bills. The only way you will ever get out of debt is to stop worrying and to start creating. In other words, you must focus on what you want, not on what you DON'T want!

Don't underestimate yourself! If someone asked you today to state your worth, what would your answer be? In what context would you even be inclined to *estimate* your worth? Most people tend to equate their personal worth with whatever material assets they possess. Had people like Aristotle Onassis been inclined to do this, their lives might have taken an entirely different turn. At the age of seventeen, Onassis left home with sixty dollars in his pocket. Had he believed this to be the true measure of his worth, it is doubtful that he would ever have gone on to build a financial empire in excess of $500 million.

You are NOT your net worth. Your real worth lies in your ability to acquire. All of your skills, your knowledge, attitudes, education, experience, and contacts are worth a great deal more than anything else you your own. *Your real bank account consists of whatever makes all the rest of it possible.* People who are truly secure know that if everything were taken away from them today, they would still have the means of getting it all back. Whatever they did once they can always do again.

DOING IT TILL YOU GET IT RIGHT

When someone pays you for the work you have performed, you are exchanging your skills and experiences for money. Every day you gain experiences that you can turn into money, and so, your earning capacity is constantly growing.

Ebb and flow times provide yet another lesson about life. Sometimes, life stops us to teach us something that must be learned before we can go on. I am inclined to believe that we set this up on an unconscious level. We continue to do a certain thing until we finally learn the lesson. We continue to go back to the same point until we get another perspective on the situation and learn how to handle it. When we are experiencing an ebb and have little money, we are learning lessons that will enable us to handle money better when it comes. In order to achieve this kind of perspective, we sometimes need to keep our lives simple, uncluttered by the distractions money brings, until we understand what needs to be done.

Take it one day at a time. Consider the actions you can take today in order to create money. You may occasionally get lost in your long-term plans and feel unnecessary pressures from them. You may even feel like a failure for not having already accomplished your dreams, but it is easy to get back on course. Simply concentrate on what you can do TODAY.

COPING WITH THE DROUGHT OF DOUBT

Almost everyone is plagued with certain doubts about money—doubts that there will be enough or that they even possess the ability to earn what is needed. People who have already amassed great fortunes are plagued with similar doubts—only on a much larger scale.

Instead of worrying about money, doesn't it make more sense to increase your self-worth and self-esteem? There is an enormous difference between these two thought patterns, since one focuses on lack and the other focuses on growth and expansion.

It is not enough to sit around and believe that things will get better. You must ACT upon your beliefs! Action is the link between wanting and getting. It is also the link between the mental and the physical world.

Your dreams exist in your mind, but they need to be brought to life through action. You will know when you are on the right path, for then, things will begin to happen! The right doors will open. The right people will come into your life, and the situations and circumstances that surround you will seem to support everything you do.

(NOTE: If you have to struggle and exert a great amount of effort to make things go right, you may be sure that you are going against the natural flow. The real test is not in how hard you try, but in how easily obstacles are overcome. There is a fine line between pushing ahead and allowing things to happen. If too much emphasis is placed on either side, you will obstruct your goals. One of the great secrets of life is to know when to push forward and when to let go. Once you have learned this, you will be well on your way to creating anything you want. Unfortunately, there is no easy way to learn or to teach this. Ultimately, the lesson is learned through personal experience and a heightened self-awareness.)

There will be times when nothing seems to be happening on the outside, but when considerable changes are taking place on the inside. At such times, keep trusting in your ability to handle what needs to be handled. It takes time for major changes to occur, and many people give up prematurely.

The bigger the goal, the bigger the change that is required. A certain number of steps will need to be taken and various events will need to occur before you can get from where you are to where you want to be.

MAKING YOUR OWN LUCK

Timing plays a very important role in every successful endeavor. If the right thing comes along at the wrong time, or if the wrong thing comes along at the right time, you will not be properly prepared. You will not be ready. The challenges of life are serious undertakings and can only be met by those who have learned how to handle their daily affairs with optimum skill.

In Ernest Hemingway's classic novel *The Old Man and the Sea*, the ancient fisherman, Santiago, has this to say: "It is better to be lucky, but I would rather be exact. Then, when luck comes, you are ready."

To be ready—with all of one's professional knowledge and expertise at hand—that is the secret to being truly prepared!

Once you feel that you are ready, step back and observe the situation with total detachment. Detachment, in this case, can be defined as a mental letting-go. If you feel that you cannot live without some specific thing in your life, eventually you will be trapped by your desire. But once you let go of the desire, you will be free to have whatever you want.

Remember too that the circumstances of your life can change at any time. The process does not take forever, unless, of course, you are convinced that it will. Undoubtedly, there have been times when you were worried about bills, when you feared losing your job or the support or affection of someone near to you. And then suddenly everything changed for the better. These are synchronistic events that occur when you let go of need and attachment and trust that life will say yes. Try it and see for yourself!

WHAT MONEY REALLY BUYS

Money is neither good nor bad. Money is just ideas in action. It is the way money is used that ultimately determines whether it will create positive or negative circumstances in your life.

It is all right to be rich. That may seem like a strange thing to say, but there are many people who feel guilty about having money because so many others are doing without.

Money enables you to help those around you. It also allows you to do what you love to do, to fulfill your life's purpose. Money is not only a means with which to purchase material things. It also buys freedom—and time. Once you have enough money, you will no longer need to sacrifice your freedom and time to things that do not support your creative intentions, or to anything that makes you unhappy or leaves you feeling unfulfilled.

Thoughts *intensified.*

Visions *dramatized.*

Lifelong dreams *realized.*

That is what money can buy.

CHAPTER 9
A Lesson From Ramon

I generally do not include case histories in my books, since I feel that they rarely serve the purpose for which they are intended. No matter what example is used, it is really the reader's own perception of any given circumstance that ultimately determines the final outcome. Even so, I have decided to make an exception for once, and in this instance, my case history will be the subject of this entire chapter. The reason for this is that I have never known anyone who more clearly exemplifies the principles discussed in this book than my friend Ramon Bonin.

I met Ramon several years ago while I was on the lecture circuit. In his continuing efforts to apply the principles for success to his own life, he came upon some of my books and tapes. At the time we first met, he was spending in excess of $6,000 annually on self-improvement material. He would even listen to my tapes while riding along in his Rolls-Royce. Over the years, he has given hundreds of my books and tapes to personal friends and business associates.

When I met his family, I realized that Ramon, his wife Patty, his son Blaise, and his daughter Kim comprised an impressive example of how a family can live by and share abundantly in the principles for success.

Through the years, it has been my privilege to know presidents, politicians, authors, celebrities, and even religious leaders, but I have never met anyone with a better grasp of the principles for personal and business success than Ramon Bonin. Here is a man who truly believes in doing what you love and loving what you do.

In a recent taped interview I conducted with Ramon, he summarized his own personal philosophy. Here, in his own words, is the way Ramon explains it:

QUES: *The first question, the obvious one, I suppose, is: Were you born with that proverbial silver spoon in your mouth?*

ANS: I was born in a backwoods region of Louisiana, in a small Cajun community where I lived with my parents in a tarpaper shack. I spoke only French until I started attending school.

QUES: *What was the extent of your formal education?*

ANS: Eleventh grade. At the time, I did not really understand the value of school. I just went because that's what everybody else did. No great value was ever placed upon education by my uneducated parents. At the age of fifteen, I decided it was time to strike out on my own.

QUES: *What did you do after that?*

ANS: I worked at menial tasks, mostly farm work in Ohio, for which I was paid the sum of fifty cents per hour.

QUES: *Would you say there were any significant influences in your life at this time?*

ANS: Yes. A retired schoolteacher who was the

mother of one of the farmers with whom I worked. It was because of her that I developed an avid interest in reading. I began to make a sincere effort to understand what each book was telling me, to discover its basic message rather than simply looking at the words. As time went on, I began to read philosophy, literature, poetry, and even after joining the navy, I continued to be an avid reader.

QUES: *Were there any books that particularly impressed you at that time?*

ANS: Yes. I remember buying a book for twenty-five cents entitled: *In Tune With The Infinite*, by Ralph Waldo Trine. That book communicated something to me that changed my entire life. Its basic overall message was that we live in a universe that is controlled by fixed laws, and one of these laws is the law of cause and effect. At the age of twenty-three, I did not immediately grasp the full impact of this, but eventually, I did. I gradually came to the realization that I was completely in charge of my destiny, that what happened to me was a result of what I did, and also, what I failed to do—my acts of commission as well as my acts of omission. Whatever occurred or did not occur, I was solely in charge.

QUES: *After your discharge from the navy, what did you do?*

ANS: I went back to performing menial tasks, common-labor-type jobs. In California I found a job as a shipping clerk that paid $1.26 per hour. Before very long, I noticed many inefficiencies in the way things were done. There was no organization, which made it extremely difficult to fill orders on a timely basis. Although I had not been invited to do it, I gradually worked out a more efficient system, and once it had been adopted, everything moved along much more smoothly. After that, I began looking at the assembly area with the same critical eye. Fortunately, I had always possessed a natural ability to look at a situation and see what needed to be done. During idle moments, I would clean up the place and rearrange things so that they would be more organized. It seemed important to establish some kind of order, perhaps because order is a very important part of my life. I also worked after-hours and helped the employees clean and set up their equipment. Eventually, I was moved to the production department and received an increase in salary.

QUES: *How goal-oriented were you in those days?*

ANS: Not at all. I had absolutely no sense of purpose. I just went to work every day because I knew I had to eat. I took a lot of menial, dead-end jobs, whatever was available.

QUES: *What do you believe was responsible for eventually altering your outlook?*

ANS: I got married. As you might expect, this had a very dramatic effect upon my life. For the very first time, I began to focus on purpose, to consider the idea of working toward something specific. I had never done that before. I had always just worked to survive. But once I was married, my wife and I became interested in owning things, in having things that would make life more comfortable and enjoyable. And this meant I needed a specific plan in order to achieve my goals. The first thing we did was move to a rural area, since neither of us had ever really enjoyed living in the city.

QUES: *Was this a fortuitous move?*

ANS: It changed everything! I went to work as a helper for a local building contractor, and that was the beginning of a beautiful lifetime career. I had never before loved my work, or even really liked it. Although I respected my employers and always did an outstanding job for them, I simply put in my hours. But when I started working for this building contractor, I found I couldn't wait to get to work! We were building custom homes, and each day, I would eagerly drive a distance of sixty miles and throw myself into my job. At the end of the day, it was the same thing in reverse. I would continue to think about my work after I returned home, wondering what we would be doing next. It was all so incredibly exciting! I absolutely loved my job!

QUES: *How would you describe your overall attitude and feelings at this time?*

ANS: As one of constant expectancy. Driving in each morning, I found I could not wait to get there. And I hated to see the day end since this meant I had to wait until the following morning to see what would happen next!

QUES: *Would you say that your relationship with*

> *your employer was a pleasant and com-*
> *patible one?*

ANS: He was more like a mentor. He was incredibly patient, was an excellent communicator, and always took the time to explain everything we were doing, and why. He was also a master craftsman and taught me to demand the best of myself in all situations. I learned all the elements of construction since he himself was involved in every phase—digging foundations, doing form work, pouring concrete, framing, all the way through to the actual finishing. By the time I returned to southern California, which I eventually did, I was well schooled and ready to take on the world!

QUES: *What did you do then?*

ANS: I went to work for a framing contractor, although he did not really want to hire me. Someone had given me his name and I went to his house and knocked on his door. When he answered, he opened the door only slightly and tried to close it again when I told him I was looking for a job. Since I desperately needed work, I couldn't afford to have him do this, so I put my hand against the door to keep him from closing it. I offered to work for him an entire week with the understanding that if I did not make him any money, he would not owe me a cent. He admitted he had never had an offer like that in his life and promptly took me on. Within three weeks, I was running his crew.

QUES: *How did you launch your career as an independent contractor?*

ANS: It came about as a result of a conversation I happened to overhear. The job superintendent asked the contractor if he would be interested in cutting some doors between offices and installing window air-conditioning units. The contractor said no, that he considered this "junk work" and that he couldn't make any money on it. So, I offered to do it myself.

QUES: *When did you find the time to do it?*

ANS: During the evenings. And on weekends. Soon other people were referring the same kind of work to me, and suddenly, I was drowning in opportunity!

QUES: *Drowning in opportunity. I like that! With that kind of an attitude, I assume you managed to stay busy?*

ANS: That was twenty-five years ago, and I've never run out of work. For the first seven years, I worked seven days a week, but after that, I began to relax, no longer fearful that I would ever be unemployed.

QUES: *What principles for success were you utilizing at this time?*

ANS: Mainly those I had learned as a child. To always be honest, and grateful, to have a good attitude, to do the best job I knew how, to communicate well, and to always keep things simple.

QUES: *Can you remember at what point you made the transition from "junk work" to major construction?*

ANS: Oh yes. I was maintaining a rigorous schedule, often working twenty-hour days in an effort to meet my projected deadlines. One day, while I was digging ditches in downtown L.A., I learned of a piece of condemned property for sale. I purchased it for $7,200 and later sold it for $15,000. After the sale was made, I was contacted by some people who wanted me to construct a building on that lot. I explained that the property had already been sold, but offered to find another site on which to erect a building. This was the start of my career as an independent developer. Utilizing what I had learned in northern California, I did all of the layout work and constructed the building in about sixty days. I did most of the work myself—dug ditches by hand, put in the forms, tied the steel, did the roof structure as well as the interior framing. I loved every minute of it! I made more money on this job in a shorter period of time than I had ever made in my life.

QUES: *Again, I must ask you, what principles for success were you applying?*

ANS: I spent a lot of time thinking about my clients—what I could do for them, what they would like. I began to come up with a lot of creative ideas and often ended up giving more than I was being paid for. At the time, I didn't recognize these practices as principles for success, but obviously they were. I did only quality work, and in my book, the customer was always right. One time, it meant painting one room four different times before the lady was finally satisfied, but afterward, she repaid me by involving me in five additional jobs.

QUES: *At that point, you had obviously begun to apply that principle of positive expectancy you were talking about.*

ANS: Oh yes. It is truly amazing how often we will succeed when we proceed on the premise that we cannot fail.

As time went on, I continued to acquire properties—single lots, at first, then two lots. After a while, it became five and six lots at a time. Eventually, it became entire city blocks, and in one case, I acquired an eleven-acre tract of land in downtown Los Angeles on which I developed 400,000 square feet of buildings. All the buildings had already been leased or sold before I even closed escrow on the land. At present, I am in the somewhat enviable position of being able to take on as much work as I want, drawing on the abundance that is always there.

QUES: *So, you are still drowning in opportunity?*

ANS: Oh yes, but I would like to stress that getting to this point was not a "happy accident." It all came about because I applied specific principles for success. In the early days, I applied them unconsciously, but now it's a deliberate process.

QUES: *So, what you are saying is you can never afford to stop learning and applying what you learn.*

ANS: That's right. In some cases, it's simply a matter of discovering what principles you have been applying accidentally, so that you can give them a label and make them a conscious part of your life. In my own case, I continued to read and started listening to motivational tapes in an effort to uncover the true principles for success.

QUES: *Are you a list maker?*

ANS: Very much so. A long time ago I got into the habit of writing down whatever it was that I wanted to accomplish. The lists are important, I think, because they make your goals more tangible.

QUES: *And once the lists were made, what did you do then?*

ANS: Then I formulated definite plans in order to achieve those goals.

QUES: *For people who might be interested in developing such plans, would you like to explain the specific steps involved?*

ANS: Well, I would define each plan in terms of how I was going to achieve my objectives. Writing it all down in outline form, I would take each topic and break it down to the smallest detail. Then I would determine what resources I would need to accomplish my plan.

QUES: *At this stage in your life, do you consider yourself a self-made man?*

ANS: Oh no. Everything I have done has taken some team effort. I realized early on that the things I wanted to accomplish couldn't be accomplished alone, because my goals were always greater than my individual capacity. So, I made a practice of surrounding myself with a group of the best-qualified people I could find.

QUES: *By most people's definition, you are certainly a successful person. In your own mind, how would you define success?*

ANS: I think success has more to do with choices than anything else—the freedom to choose what it is you want to do in life and having the resources to pursue those choices, whatever those resources might be. If I were to define a successful life, I would have to say it is different for each and every one of us. Too often, people tend to equate success with money, or the acquisition of wealth.

While I believe that can be *part* of success, the real success lies in finding what you love to do and having the freedom to do it. What a beautiful feeling that is, to pursue this thing you love to do and to have it as your job.

QUES: *In other words, what you are really saying is, if you really love what you're doing, you'll never work another day in your life.*

ANS: Exactly! I don't remember working a single day since I first found the thing I truly love to do. I just look forward to daily challenges and accomplishments.

QUES: *What about people who have nothing, no money to speak of? Do you think the acquisition of wealth is a good motivation for them?*

ANS: Well, as we already know, money is not the answer to everything. If it were, wealthy people would be totally ecstatic, and we know this is far from true. By the same token, those who are relatively poor, at least from a financial standpoint, are often very happy and well adjusted, particularly if they feel they have a real mission in life, and if they truly enjoy whatever it is they are doing.

QUES: *What about people who don't really know what they want to do?*

ANS: I would tell anyone who made that state-

ment: "You're making your life too difficult." You see, it really isn't a matter of
finding the one thing that's *perfect*, but
finding whatever seems best at the time.
I would think that if someone didn't know
exactly what they wanted to do, that they
could begin by making a list of various
things that had always interested them.
The important thing here is to jot down
whatever occurs to you, without regard
for possible difficulties or limitations.
Just make out the list, and then, through
a process of elimination, determine which
thing or things appeal to you the most.
Eventually, you are going to get down to
a very small group of choices, which
should clearly indicate what you should
actually be doing. Another way is to not
focus on the job at all, but rather on the
activities and conditions you most like to
surround yourself with. This, in itself,
will suggest the kind of work you should
be doing.

QUES: *And, assuming these people have the
proper attitudes and behavior patterns,
what else do you think they will need in
order to succeed?*

ANS: There are certain basic laws of nature,
and one of the most dominant ones is that
all things find their own level. If you place
a person in an environment that is totally
alien to his nature, only one of two things
can possibly happen. Either he will separate himself from that environment, or
else he will *become* like the environment.
This is a particularly significant fact to
consider when a person with limited

skills and abilities is placed in a situation where something clearly superior is expected of him. In order to make the adjustment, it becomes necessary for him to aspire to something higher in order to succeed in that environment. The important thing to learn from this is that if you wish to improve in life, you must first place yourself in an improved environment.

QUES: *What about the PEOPLE you choose to surround yourself with?*

ANS: It's all the same thing. If you wish to succeed, you will need to associate with people who think on a higher level, who have higher principles, and who communicate in a truly positive way. In other words, people with higher ideals.

QUES: *In your dealings with people, it appears that you subscribe to the win-win philosophy. Is that true?*

ANS: Definitely! The cause of a lot of failure in life is the erroneous idea that you have to get *more*, that "winning" means getting a bigger piece of the pie. This is untrue. Although you may, in fact, get a bigger piece of the pie, it may well be the only pie you'll ever get. Practicing the win-win philosophy is simply a matter of helping *others* to win. Not only that, it also means never participating in any activity that is not conducive to a win-win situation. One of the major elements of success is helping other people get what they want. In order to do that, you have to make sure that they win, and that they *feel* they have won, according to their own individual perceptions of winning. It is only when people feel they have won that they will come back to you so that you can help them to win again.

QUES: *It appears obvious to me, from what I have personally observed, that no matter what happens to you, you always subscribe to an Attitude of Gratitude. Would you say that is a fair assessment?*

ANS: Yes, very much so, You've undoubtedly heard the saying: *Happiness is not having what you want, but wanting what you have.* An Attitude of Gratitude falls right in harmony with that. There are so many people who have true abundance, but who nonetheless persist in focusing on the little that is wrong, rather than on everything that is right.

Through the years, I've created something I call Ramon's Rule, and I use the standard yardstick as a metaphor. In every yardstick you will find exactly thirty-six inches. Everyone has a yardstick of life, and in each life there are so many inches of good conditions, and so many inches of bad. Some people, who are blessed with thirty-five inches of good and only one inch of bad, choose to focus on their one bad inch, and eventually, their whole life becomes bad. If you focus on the bad, it becomes your reality. Since your thoughts produce your feelings, if your thoughts are bad, then your feelings will be bad, and the quality of your life will also be bad. This is the best reason I can think of to concentrate on what is good about your life. An Attitude of Gratitude is something I have always been blessed with. No matter what my job is, no matter how lowly a task it might be, I always appreciate having a job, which is no small thing in itself.

QUES: *Good point! Now then, let's talk about results. You already know from reading my books and listening to my tapes that I am results oriented. How do you feel about that?*

ANS: Well, we are all inclined to seek out people who are going to help us get what we want. Whether we're looking for a mechanic to fix our car or someone to type a letter for us, we are looking for someone who can provide what we need.

That's what success is all about— knowing what you need to do and when you need to do it. Many people in this world possess the potential for success. They have skills and motivation, long-term goals, and even the proper attitude. But they never quite get around to doing what they NEED to do when they need to DO it. In other words, they go through the motions, but never achieve the results. Faulty timing is often a big part of their problem. If you have critical deadlines to meet and somehow don't meet them, you only create additional problems. Like you have repeatedly said: *There are reasons and there are results.* Results are all that matter. Excuses don't count.

QUES: *How do you feel about proper timing, about being in the right place at the right time?*

ANS: I think the time is now! The time is always. I think that timing is really a matter of mental attitude. Success is not so much a matter of overcoming the wrong conditions as overcoming whatever conditions exist. Let's not forget that there are many people who will fail even under the best conditions, while others, who are constantly battling adversity, somehow manage to rise above their conditions and achieve great success.

QUES: *Which leads us finally to the subject of integrity, this business of living up to your word. How important do you believe this is in your dealings with others?*

ANS: I would say integrity is vital to your success, that any kind of *long-term* success is impossible without it. Also, there is tremendous power in being predictable in a positive way. What many people don't realize is that we all evaluate patterns of behavior in others. If a pattern of behavior is good, if promises are kept and work is performed according to the terms and conditions originally agreed upon, you may be sure that you will always be surrounded with satisfied customers. On the other hand, there are many people who will say what they are going to do and then change it in varying degrees as time goes on. Although they may believe this is an acceptable practice, it is not. Predictability is extremely important as it pertains to integrity. It is never wise to "change the game." Never!

QUES: *Would you agree that the bottom line for making all the principles for success work*

*is your own self-image and your sense of
self-esteem?*

ANS: Yes, definitely. We all have a picture of
ourselves, which I sometimes refer to as
our "script." We all have a particular perception of how life is and how *we* are.
There is a scripture in the Bible that
reads: *As you believe in your heart, so
shall it be done unto you.* I think that
covers the self-image and self-esteem situation pretty well. It isn't so much what
happens but how we *feel* about what happens that makes the difference. When we
have a poor self-image and poor self-
esteem, we have a tendency to react badly
to the situations we encounter. Life is a
miracle! What we put into it is what
comes back to us, and the manner in
which we respond to situations in our
lives will determine in large measure
how other people regard us. If we are rude
and arrogant, it is unlikely that anyone
will ever treat us kindly. And if we are
dishonest, people will certainly not be
motivated to do business with us. But if
we are considerate and caring, and exhibit a winning attitude, we will make it
far more desirable for others to interact
with us.

QUES: *And finally, to sum things up, would you
like to share any closing thoughts that others might find helpful as they undertake
their own road to success?*

ANS: I would say the single most important realization that any of us can ever come to
is that we are totally responsible for ourselves and everything that happens to us.

We live in a universe that is governed by
fixed laws, such as the law of cause and
effect. Whether we believe in such laws
or not will not alter the fact that they
exist. It is like the law of gravity. If a
person decides to walk off a cliff, the fact
that he does not believe in the law of gravity will not alter the fact that he will fall.
Getting back to cause and effect, it is important to understand that you are de-
signing your destiny each day—with
every act you commit or *fail* to commit.
Because the things you do in the present
have such an impact upon the future, an
effort should be made to choose the destiny you really want. The next step is to
do something *each day* that will bring you
a little closer to your objective, however
inconsequential an act it may appear to
be. The important thing is to keep moving
ahead, with your eye on the target.

And finally, never, never, *never* give
up! There are many people who succeed
in life, not because they are more intelligent, more educated, or better qualified
than others, but because they *refuse to
fail!* They never quit. They never let go.
They push and persevere, until finally,
they have no choice but to win! Better to
be a person who tried and failed than
someone who *failed to try.* Always try.
Always believe in yourself. And enjoy
every day that you live!

CHAPTER 10
What To Do When You Don't Know What To Do

Not knowing how to do something should never be accepted as a legitimate reason for not doing it—particularly when the thing you are NOT doing is the thing you really love!

This chapter is dedicated to those who do not know what they would like to be doing, and also, to those who DO know, but who see no way of realizing their goal.

In order to help as many people as possible, we will use a hypothetical case study involving a young lady we will refer to as Margaret Ann Potter.

Maggie, as she will be informally addressed, is presently employed as an administrative assistant to a highly successful real-estate developer. While she takes pride in doing her job well, she is not happy in her work, although certain aspects of it occasionally appeal to her. In addition to her basic secretarial duties, she is occasionally invited to make suggestions on promotional brochures and other advertising material that her employer uses in order to publicize his new projects. In the past, Maggie has helped him write these brochures and ads, and she regularly handles all of his correspondence, composing it herself once the basic message has been conveyed to her.

Maggie is obviously drawn to any aspect of her job that concerns writing. Everything else is of little interest to her.

Whenever she is asked what she would prefer to do if any career were available to her, Maggie appears uncertain.

"I like to write," she admits. "In school, I thoroughly enjoyed my English and journalism classes. And also, our Thespian society. Occasionally, we would present original plays, and I very much enjoyed working on those."

While it is clear that Maggie would like to do something that involves writing, there remains the question of *what* she should do and how she should go about doing it.

Maggie has no illusions about what it takes to become a professional writer. She knows writing is a skill that is gradually developed and refined, and that she will have to serve an apprenticeship. Meanwhile, life goes on and bills must be paid. Better to forget about writing, Maggie decides, since it is more important to be practical. But somehow, being practical is not enough. Maggie soon realizes that the nagging discontent she feels is not going to go away. This forces her, at last, to consider taking on some sort of work connected with writing. For the time being, she knows it will need to be a part-time occupation.

Maggie writes down everything she can think of that is even remotely related to this field. The things that come immediately to mind are put on one sheet of paper, then the less obvious possibilities are listed on another sheet. In time, there is a third sheet, on which is listed a *combination* of her thoughts.

It takes Maggie seven days to complete her lists. When the first two lists have been combined to make the third, it reads something like this:

Public-relations work
Resume writing
Technical writing
Speech writing
Business correspondence/home-based
   secretarial service
Advertising work
Newspaper reporting (stringer)
Newspaper-column writing
Ghostwriting
Book reviewer
Newsletter service
Novelist
Screenwriter

Offshoots:

Proofreading
Editing
Research work

Once the final list is complete, Maggie is surprised at the number of choices actually available to her. Now, it is simply a matter of eliminating those that are the least desirable. Once this is done, Maggie's list is reduced to:

Newsletter service
Advertising work
Ghostwriting
Novelist

Of the choices that remain, Maggie is now ready to admit that she wishes to be a successful novelist more than anything else in the world! She also knows that advertising work, newsletter writing, and ghostwriting will assist her in achieving her goal.

In the town where Maggie lives, there is a weekly newspaper, the *Legal & Business Gazette*, that regularly prints a listing of all the new business telephones that have recently been installed. Taking note of these numbers and addresses, Maggie pays a visit to the owner of each establishment. She is not surprised to find that while these people are certainly interested in advertising their products and services, they cannot afford the fees being charged by major agencies in town. Once Maggie has determined what each potential customer can afford to spend, she agrees to work for them for a regular monthly retainer.

In time, Maggie's little business grows to the point where she can afford to work independently on a full-time basis. A newsletter service soon adds to the volume of work she regularly performs under the name of Action Advertising.

Throughout this period, Maggie gradually learns of various writers' groups in town. She becomes a member of those that have the most to offer and attends their monthly meetings. She also advertises in their newsletters, offering proofreading, editing, and typing services.

Maggie is pleased with her progress, since the people with whom she is now associating are in a field she truly enjoys. She is socializing and working with other writers—and best of all, she is *learning* from them!

As her skills become more polished, she takes on some major rewriting work. Her clients are pleased with her ability to make some sense out of their poorly structured plots. This inevitably leads to her first professional ghostwriting assignment, and with the help of a well-placed ad in the Sunday edition of the newspaper, other such assignments quickly follow.

At this point, Maggie is ready to phase herself out of advertising work and become a full-time writer. She works on a performance-contract basis, collecting portions of her fee as each job progresses. Meanwhile, she is thinking seriously about writing a book of her own.

Because of her commitments to others, Maggie soon finds that her own book rarely receives the time and attention it deserves. While it seems at first that there are just not enough hours in the day, she senses that she is really procrastinating.

One day, Maggie realizes that it is time to face the situation squarely. She makes a point of reminding herself that everything she has done thus far is in the interest of furthering her own writing career. It is time to begin her novel! She knows she must work on it with the same amount of diligence and dedication that she has always applied when working for others.

Once again, it is necessary to formulate a plan and commit herself to a specific schedule. When it is done, it looks like this:

WRITING GOAL (Subject Matter):_____

_____

Pages per day _____ = ___1___ chapter every _____

Deadline dates:

Chapter 1	_____	Chapter 11	_____
Chapter 2	_____	Chapter 12	_____
Chapter 3	_____	Chapter 13	_____
Chapter 4	_____	Chapter 14	_____
Chapter 5	_____	Chapter 15	_____
Chapter 6	_____	Chapter 16	_____
Chapter 7	_____	Chapter 17	_____
Chapter 8	_____	Chapter 18	_____
Chapter 9	_____	Chapter 19	_____
Chapter 10	_____	Chapter 20	_____

First draft completion date:

_____

Time allotted for editing, proofing, revision:

_____

Second draft completion date:

_____

Third draft completion date:

_____

DEADLINE DATE SET FOR MAILING:

_____

Working according to this schedule, Maggie is pleased to find her book progressing nicely. Once it is completed, she sends it off to an agent and then thinks about other short- and long-term goals. Not *all* of her goals are concerned with writing, but in every case, they involve something she would like to change or improve in her life. At this point, Maggie is ready to make up a *perpetual* list of goals. As each one is achieved, she intends to cross it off and then add on another. The format for this list is quite simple in design:

GOAL #1 _____

How I intend to achieve this goal_____

_____

_____

Deadline date_____

GOAL #2 _____

How I intend to achieve this goal _____

_____

_____

Deadline date _____

GOAL #3 _____

How I intend to achieve this goal _____

_____

_____

Deadline date _____

GOAL #4 _____

How I intend to achieve this goal _____

_____

_____

Deadline date _____

GOAL #5 _____

How I intend to achieve this goal _____

_____

_____

Deadline date _____

Maggie decides that she should always have a list of five projected goals, as this is a comfortable number for her. She begins at once to work toward each of them, paying careful attention to her progress.

The foregoing case study involving Margaret Ann Potter is easily adapted to other individuals and professions. In each instance, the steps involved are the same:

STEP #1

Make up two lists of possible career choices. The first will be done on a totally conscious level. The second will consist of ideas that come to you more spontaneously. Finally, there will be a third list, which is actually a composite of the former two. A period of seven days should be devoted to each individual list.

STEP #2

By eliminating all of the less desirable choices on your final list, you will soon be able to determine the thing or things you would most like to do.

STEP #3

If your immediate financial obligations do not permit you to undertake your life's work on a full-time basis, you should begin to work TOWARD it in a way that at least allows you to become involved in some related field.

(NOTE: In Maggie's case, she began to do advertising

work. While copywriting was not the writing she most
enjoyed, it was *writing* as opposed to waitressing or clerk-
ing. It was closer to what she wanted to do than any other
job she had ever held.)

STEP #4

Seek out the company of those who are already successful in the field you wish to enter. For a time, you may
wish to work *for* them, or possibly, become affiliated with
them through their clubs and organizations. This is one
of the easiest ways to begin working toward your long-
range goal. It works like cross-pollination in the sense
that you will constantly be picking up and tossing out
valuable ideas and, in this way, continue to learn from
the experts in your field.

STEP #5

Once you have begun to work toward your goal, it is
important to remind yourself that you are really *working
toward it!* Every day. In every way. As quickly as possible, eliminate anything that causes you to veer off your
path, anything that draws you into activities totally un-
related to your life's work.

STEP #6

Design your master plan! This is the really BIG one,
the one you have been working toward from the first.
Write down the exact steps involved in achieving this
goal, as well as anticipated deadline dates. Then keep
this schedule in front of you! Look at it the first thing
every morning and the last thing every night. Allow your-

self to feel pressured by your self-imposed demands. Take time to enjoy the exhilarating tension that is causing you to work harder—and *smarter!*

STEP #7

Make up a second list of short- and long-term goals, those related to both personal and professional matters. As each goal is achieved, add on yet another, and keep the cycle going!

STEP #8

Reward yourself for what you have accomplished. Treat yourself to an evening on the town, to a special little gift (nothing practical, please!) or a well-deserved vacation. Permit yourself to feel proud of what you have done, and what you are presently doing.

STEP #9

Keep doing it!

STEP #10

Finally, allow yourself the ultimate luxury of doing what you love and loving what you do!

DON'T DELAY! GET UNDERWAY! TODAY!

The only difference between those who devise a way to perform their life's work and those who do *not* should be altogether obvious by now. There is nothing in this chapter, or even in this entire book, that has not been successfully tested and proven to be a workable concept— either by myself or by other successful people I have known. *These methods work!* The only way they *cannot* work is if they are not applied. Step 1 must, of logic and necessity, inevitably lead to Step 2. From that point on, each step will lead you to the next—as long as you are willing to persevere.

Nothing unreasonable is expected of you! Never, under any circumstances, are you ever encouraged to abandon any gainful means of employment. Nothing impulsive or foolhardy is required. Nothing of that kind is even necessary.

The real object here is to get you working TOWARD your goals, whatever will make you feel happy and fulfilled. In order to get where you are going, you must first undertake the journey! You are reading this book because you want to live life as it was *meant* to be lived. There is nothing wrong with that!

If I could sit down and speak with you personally, the things I would say would most certainly include everything that is contained within these pages. To that, I can only add that I know you are capable of achieving whatever you wish. I know you possess the talent, the skills, and the potential. And certainly, the opportunities are there. Opportunities are everywhere!

START WITH ENTHUSIASM

A happier, more successful life is the product of both a creative and a decisive mind. In the end, there is only one way to begin to improve your thoughts, your attitudes, your life! The way to do it is to simply *start doing it!* The way to think for yourself is to start thinking for yourself. Are you beginning to get the idea? Good!

Whatever you do, do it with enthusiasm! Enthusiasm is that very special something that makes us great, that pulls us out of the mediocre and commonplace, that gives us power and a special glow and shine. People respond positively to an enthusiastic person, someone who is not a deadbeat but a producer, someone who is ready to take on the world! Enthusiasm will put spring in your step and confidence in your heart.

Try to remember that progress begins with the belief that there is no better person in all the world than YOU! So always be yourself. Remember! As long as you are being yourself, no one can ever accuse you of doing it wrong.

A PERSONAL-PROGRESS CHART

Having made the decision to undertake your life's work, you will undoubtedly find the first year to be an exceptionally exciting and challenging one. You may wish to monitor your progress and take special note of areas that need improvement. If so, the following chart will prove extremely helpful:

PERSONAL PROGRESS CHART

Grading system: A—No improvement needed
B—Little improvement needed
C—Some improvement needed
D—Substantial improvement needed
F—Major improvement needed

SUBJECT	Present	6 mo.	12 mo.
Ability to accept responsibility	————	————	————
Sense of purpose—specific goals set	————	————	————
Persistence	————	————	————
Self-discipline and motivation	————	————	————
Ability to make and act upon decisions	————	————	————
Ability to reinforce self	————	————	————
Ability to set priorities	————	————	————
Enjoyment of work	————	————	————
Belief in ability to succeed	————	————	————

Time-manage-
ment skills   _____   _____   _____

Ability to meet
deadlines   _____   _____   _____

Ability to avoid
unnecessary de-
mands upon one's
time   _____   _____   _____

Ability to organize
smooth work flow   _____   _____   _____

Energy level   _____   _____   _____

Degree of sincerity   _____   _____   _____

Overall attitude   _____   _____   _____

A SENSE OF URGENCY

Your lists, your schedules and charts will make everything you do that pertains to your life's work seem that
much more important. Before very long, this feeling will
escalate into a sense of urgency! In case you hadn't already guessed, that's the whole idea!

Many people are avid readers of motivational books.
They also listen to tapes. Whenever possible, they may
attend lectures and give thoughtful consideration to the
success formulas that others have used. Still, they never
get into high gear!

Something you must understand about success-oriented information, regardless of its form, is that *it will never rub off.* Nothing will happen until you are ready to apply what you've learned! Reading about success is a passive exercise. So is listening to tapes. In order for anything to work for you, you must first become actively involved!

As you begin to feel a greater sense of urgency about your life's work, you begin to make lists and formulate your plans and schedules. *Now* you are in an active rather than a passive mode. *Now* you are applying the things you have learned as you itemize your goals and work out a method for achieving them. *Now* you are engaged in the Law of Sow and Reap:

- Wherever you happen to be—START FROM THERE.
- Visualize the life you have always wanted to lead.
- Design a plan of action that is uniquely your own.
- Believe in your plan and in yourself.
- Have faith in a Higher Power.
- Have courage. And confidence.
- Then GO FOR IT!

CHAPTER 11
Power Thoughts To Get You Started

When you first begin working toward any major goal, it is important to surround yourself with as many positive people and situations as you can draw into your life. You should always gravitate toward whatever is most compatible to your dream. It is equally important to control your own thoughts, to keep them as positive and uplifting as you can. Thoughts are forces that will either work *for* you or *against* you. For this reason, it is necessary to stand guard over them, to make certain that your thoughts are always supportive of your dreams.

In addition to investing in motivational books and tapes, it is essential that you begin each day in the proper frame of mind. One way of doing this is to give yourself an inspiring *Thought for the Day,* something to think about as you perform you daily tasks, something to keep you focused on your long-range goals. As time goes on, you will undoubtedly compose a number of your own, but just to get you started, here is a month's supply of positive and thought-provoking messages.

DEVELOP A POSITIVE FAITH IN YOURSELF

Doing what you love and loving what you do requires that you develop *positive* faith in yourself. Successful people tend to share this trait. One of the best ways to begin seeing yourself in a positive light is to visualize yourself as you want to be. Positive statements and affirmations are also important, of course, and each message should be carefully evaluated before you allow it to enter your subconscious mind.

KILLER PHRASES	*CREATIVE PHRASES*
I have to	I want to
I can't	I can
If only	Next time
Difficult	Challenging
Problem	Opportunity
I'll try	I will
I have to	I choose to
Eventually I should	Right now I will

ELIMINATE PROCRASTINATION

Procrastination is another word for fear. It may well be a fear of failure or a fear that you may not succeed. Perfectionists are often master procrastinators; they choose to do nothing rather than to risk the possibility of doing something wrong. Procrastinators fear the unknown, they fear looking foolish, and may even fear success.

Life is a risky business and there is no way of knowing what may happen next. The only way out of your fear is to DO something; never become immobilized by your fears.

Also, stop thinking in terms of "have to" and tell yourself instead that you "choose to." Choices are much more pleasant to ponder and are easier to act upon.

LIFE IS NOT A COMPROMISE

Work for something you really want, not something that is a compromise. Compromises rarely will be exciting enough to stimulate you into action.

You will always be motivated to create the things you love. As you become accustomed to creating what you want, you will find that each new thing comes easier than the one before. Most things will come to you through normal channels. As your skills evolve, you will discover new techniques that will make it easier for you to acquire whatever it is you want. After a while, it may seem that you are doing little or nothing at all to draw good fortune to you. By then, through the power of your own thought processes, you will have set certain universal forces into motion that will continue to supply you abundantly.

THE PAST DOESN'T HAVE TO CONTROL YOUR FUTURE

The person you are is the result of past programming. The pain you experience is the result of trying to live with old beliefs that no longer work today.

Giving up the past is the key to inner freedom. We must come to a point where we no longer let previous programming rule our lives. The problem is, long after we have removed ourselves from those who did the original programming, we continue to allow their rules or injunctions to control our lives.

Remaining a slave to past conditioning is a choice. Refusing to be enslaved is another choice. You can redirect your life as soon as you decide you are "sick and tired of being sick and tired." It is simply a matter of clinging to the past or allowing yourself to be free.

LEARN FROM YOUR MISTAKES

None of us likes to make mistakes, and yet we all have—and will. Look at it this way: a hundred years from now, no one will even know or care. Fear of making mistakes is founded on the erroneous assumption that we need to "look good" at all times.

Isn't it far more important to learn from past mistakes? What have they taught you about living successfully? Once you see that mistakes are actually *teachers,* you can allow yourself to profit from them, and then dismiss them from your mind. If you find it difficult to release yourself from your mistakes, it simply means you have never learned how to forgive yourself. The way to do this is to separate yourself from your behavior. You are not what you DO, and you are not what you HAVE. If you believe that you are, you will always feel inferior to someone who does or has *more*.

Learn to put a statute of limitations on past mistakes, a date and time beyond which you choose never to think about them again. It's a simple idea, but it works!

THE IMPORTANCE OF GIVING AND RECEIVING

Giving is the other side of receiving. Giving of your time, abilities, and money starts a circulation of energy that will return to you as it fulfills its cycle. Whether you choose to believe it or not, the only way to create more is to give more. In order to get something, you must first give something. Whenever there is something you want, you should ask yourself: What can I give in order to get it? Remember, everything has its price.

DON'T GET CAUGHT IN THE COMPARISON TRAP

As you become more successful, it is important to surround yourself with successful people. Never allow yourself to feel inferior to them. Nor should you feel jealous or threatened. Instead, *learn* from these people! They all have valuable lessons to teach you.

A competitive personality is not a hindrance, but you must know who to compete against. Never compete against others. Always compete against yourself.

Refuse to be concerned with what others are doing, for *whatever* they are doing, their methods are undoubtedly much different from your own. Different—not necessarily better. No one can take your ideas away, if they truly ARE your ideas. And no one can put them to work in the unique way that you can. There will never be another you!

YOU DON'T HAVE TO BE A WORKAHOLIC TO BE SUCCESSFUL

Be willing to work hard, but never become a workaholic. Workaholics are motivated by fear. They are constantly anxious, aggressive, and stressed. They also tend to feel inadequate and suffer from poor self-esteem. Work provides them with an addictive high similar to those experienced by any substance abuser. Those who are obsessed with work have no time to confront unresolved personal problems generally associated with family and friends. Work pressures and responsibilities make it impossible for them to deal with their inability to solve such problems, most of which are the product of their own inability to be closer to those they love. Workaholics are incapable of creative, spontaneous forms of expression which are always blocked off by tension and stress. Small wonder that they turn out more "quantity" than "quality" work, and that others seldom, if ever, appreciate their efforts.

FOCUS ON WHAT YOU WANT INSTEAD OF WHAT YOU DON'T WANT

Focus on creating what you want, not on getting rid of what you *don't* want. Many people do not know what they want, but are altogether clear on what they DON'T want.

For every undesirable condition that exists in your life, you must be able to visualize something you hope to replace it with.

Example: Instead of saying, "I don't want to have to struggle with paying bills all the time," set up a schedule that will ensure you pay your bills easily each month.

PERFECTIONISM IS NOT A POSITIVE TRAIT

Perfectionism is a sign of low self-esteem. It is based on a childhood need for approval. The perfectionist child feels he will never get the approval he desires unless he does exactly what others expect of him. As an adult, he unconsciously looks to others as substitute parents.

The perfectionist is a peoplepleaser and is exhausted most of the time from playing a game he can never win. Whenever he attempts to relax, he feels guilty because he is not fulfilling his role as the perfect child.

The bottom line is that *there is no way to be perfect*. Nor is there any reason to be. It is far more important to retain a degree of humanness and sensitivity in life, to occasionally be vulnerable, and to allow yourself the freedom to make mistakes. You'll sleep a lot better, and you'll have a lot more friends.

PLACE A VALUE ON YOURSELF AND YOUR SERVICES

In business, it is important to receive what your services are worth. If you do not place a high enough value on your time and talents, neither will anyone else.

Many capable people never have money because they are not really clear on what their services are worth. They hope that other people will see their value and give them more than they are inclined to charge. This rarely works, as other people tend to respond to whatever image you project to them.

Another common fallacy about earning money is that it is best to reduce your fees in order to get more clients. This is going against the basic principle of creating money. If you cut your fee, you cut your flow. You are really telling your subconscious mind that your work is not worth very much, which will cause you to attract people who are inclined to support that belief. Also, the big opportunities you need in order to get ahead will never be presented to you. They will go to others who have greater confidence in their own value.

(NOTE: People prefer to deal with those who are already successful. They would rather not undertake the responsibility of *making* you successful. It is up to YOU to do that!)

ELIMINATE THE "SHOULD-OUGHT" SYNDROME FROM YOUR LIFE

The "should-ought" syndrome is tied to the expectations others have programmed in us. It forces us to concentrate on what others want for us, rather than on what we want for ourselves.

Once you become aware of what it is you really want to do, you will begin to reject what others think you "should" or "ought" to be doing.

There is no denying that our parents' behaviors, choices, and attitudes helped to mold our childhood perceptions and beliefs. In time, each of us managed to turn those beliefs into "shoulds." We came to accept that we *should* do this and we *should* do that, thereby crippling our own ability to function as free-thinking individuals.

In later life, it is important to break out of this syndrome and become more creative and independent. Why? Because it is the only way in which you will *ever* be able to do what you love and love what you do.

LEARN THE TRUE VALUE OF MONEY

Most people think that having more money will make their lives better or easier. They associate money with a greater feeling of aliveness, with well-being, self-esteem, love, inner peace, self-confidence, power, and security. Most people think that having enough money will free them from worry and enable them to relax and play. The truth is, you can enjoy many of these advantages in life without being rich.

The secret is to start *feeling* those things before you have the money. Once you learn how to create these feelings, your attitude toward money will immediately change. You will realize that you are now free to have all the money you want, because even without it, you still have the ability to feel satisfied and truly alive. Money, as many of us already know, often makes life more *complex*. If you prefer to keep it simple, then you will need to create another environment. You CAN do it—with or without money.

YOU ARE ALREADY SELF-CONFIDENT

Although much is written on the subject of self-fidence and how to attain it, the truth is, you already possess it. You were endowed with self-confidence at birth. If you doubt this, take a moment to observe the actions and reactions of most children. Before their minds become cluttered with fears and inhibitions, they express themselves honestly and do the things that make them happy. They approach life with a feeling of entitlement. Yes, children have natural confidence and courage. They believe in themselves and in their ability to accomplish whatever they set out to do. Remember that feeling? The really important thing is to *keep* remembering it, to constantly rekindle that feeling until it is once again an active part of your life.

DEFINE WHAT WORK MEANS TO YOU

The word *work* means different things to different people. The Lebanese poet Kahlil Gibran has written that "work is love made visible." Can the work you are presently doing be defined in this way?

All of us want the work we do to bring us prosperity and enable us to express ourselves. *That is as it should be.* But many people find themselves working at unpleasant and unrewarding tasks. They are unhappy, dissatisfied. In a sense, this is good, since negative emotions often encourage us to aim higher.

You can begin the search for fulfilling work by thinking of yourself as a human dynamo of concentrated, creative energy that is constantly seeking new avenues of expression. It's true, you know! That is what you are. All that remains is to find the proper outlet for your energies and talents. If you already know what that is, you are truly blessed!

DESIRE—THE MOST POWERFUL TOOL FOR CHANGE

There is nothing halfway about desire. It is intense and powerful. If properly nurtured, desire always provides the necessary fuel for success. The stronger your desire, the greater your power to produce whatever it is you want.

The best way to channel desire is toward one major goal at a time. As each is achieved, a number of small goals will generally be achieved as well. Think of desire as a higher level of consciousness that is knocking at your door, trying to give you a greater good. Trust that it exists, and that it is constantly working for you in an effort to help you succeed.

ARE YOU AN ACTOR OR A REACTOR?

Before you can perform efficiently, you must learn to think clearly. Thinking clearly, or even thinking at all, can be a difficult task.

Bear in mind that there are basically two kinds of people in this world—those who *act*, and those who *react*. Reactors do not take the time to think. They do not clearly define the real issue involved or analyze it objectively. They never take the time to separate themselves from the problem, and they rarely think in terms of viable solutions. They simply react.

Based on the foregoing, would you say that you are more inclined to *act* or *react*?

NEVER LOOK BACK

Never look back. Never belabor past mistakes or failures. Keep moving ahead. You do this by *looking* ahead and by thinking in a positive way.

Consider the dilemma of a commissioned salesperson whose volume of sales has suddenly fallen off. For the most part, he is a star performer, but now he is experiencing a lull. In his immediate situation, he would undoubtedly be inclined to ask himself: What am I doing wrong?

Actually, it is the *question* that is wrong. It would be far better if he were to ask himself: What was I doing when I was doing it *right?*

When times are difficult, it is extremely important to continue to identify with success rather than failure, since this is the only way in which you will ever get yourself moving again.

BECOME MORE FLEXIBLE AND SPONTANEOUS

In order to remain spontaneous and flexible in your thinking, try to avoid habits, particularly the more ineffectual ones.

Now and again, it is good to look at your daily routines to see how they can be improved. The object here is to expend your time and energies in only the most practical and productive ways.

(NOTE: A little reorganization in this area of your life could literally save you hours each day!)

If you would like to determine exactly how flexible and spontaneous you are, you might try the following experiment. Tomorrow morning, don't start your day as you usually do. If you tend to follow a set routine, change a few things around. Comb your hair before you wash your face. Brush your teeth before you shower. Notice how hard it is to change the manner in which you perform even small, inconsequential tasks. What does this tell you about rigid and inflexible thinking? How spontaneous and adaptable to new ideas do you think you really are?

LIVING YOUR DREAM

Try to see the difference between dreaming your life and living your dream. In the first instance, you are merely enveloped in a fantasy. Since you have no deliberate plan of action, nothing will ever happen. Dreams are attainable, but always at a price.

If you are concerned about the price that life may exact from you, you should know that a price will be paid in either case—if you choose to pursue your dream, and also, if you don't. Which price would you rather pay?

NOTHING IS CERTAIN

The only thing that is certain in life is that nothing is certain. Everything is constantly changing, which means that you must learn to be extremely flexible in your planning.

While you should always have goals, and while you should always attempt to enjoy life, it is important to understand that things may not come about in exactly the way you had planned and the end result might be something quite different from what you expected. This is not necessarily bad, even if some form of loss is involved. It is best to think of short-term losses as small battles rather than wars. Learn from them and then move on. Don't identify with any negative event. Don't even think of it in terms of good or bad. Just think of it as a situation that exists—for now. Everything changes, remember? Are you beginning to see the advantages in change?

ACCEPT YOUR PRESENT REALITY

Properly assessing reality is essential to your overall success and well-being. A realist is a person who bases his life on facts as they exist—not on conditions as he imagines or wishes them to be.

The biggest problem most people have with reality is that they make it too personal. However they regard it or feel about it, it always seems to have something to do with their own likes and dislikes. We tend to reject reality when it does not fit our own particular scheme of things, when it is unpleasant or difficult. Still, things are what they are, and how*ever* they are, there is always a way to make reality work for you. Reality is sure to have some beneficial influence upon your life, if you allow it to. Reality has taught you many things in the past. It *always* teaches you. It never deludes you in the way that impractical, theoretical, or utopian ideas are inclined to do. There is nothing to be gained from being deluded. Be realistic! In the long run, it is the easiest way.

HANDLING OBSTACLES

According to an old saying, Chaos often breeds life, when order breeds habit. Or to put it another way, pity the poor pedigreed dog, who misses the stimulus of fleas.

It goes without saying that if we could have things as we would like them to be, we would all prefer a calm and peaceful existence. Still, there is need for periodic turmoil. It challenges us. It forces us out of our apathetic

state, out of the delusion that everything is safe and secure. More than that, it forces us to become self-reliant,
something we may well have lost our knack for.

We can ill afford to lose our ability to persevere and
survive. There abilities brought us our first successes,
and they will make future successes. You cannot really
lose anything you have until you lose your *ability* to have;
perseverance makes everything possible.

CREATING YOUR INNER ENVIRONMENT

Much has been written about the need to create the
proper environment for success. Environment is a factor
worth considering, although I do not think it is as important a factor in success as others do.

To begin with, environment will only make the person
if the person has no part in shaping the environment.
Have you ever known someone who was able to alter the
entire atmosphere of a room simply by entering it? Such
people are said to have magnetic personalities—or char-
isma. The thing they actually have is an ability to influence their environment.

What do you suppose it is that makes it possible for
people to survive concentration-camp experiences, or
lengthy prison sentences, or the tortures and degradation
that are commonly experienced by prisoners of war? Had
these people allowed their environment to influence
them, they almost certainly would have been destroyed.
As it was, they withstood the discomforts and pain, but
kept some part of themselves separated from that. Always, there was a part of them that refused to exist in
that environment, that transcended their immediate situation and existed somewhere else. This is something

that all of us can do, even as we work at reshaping our environment in some positive way.

Think of the pleasant, upbeat people you have known in jobs that left a great deal to be desired. Invariably, there was someone—perhaps it was you—who made the situation more tolerable than it might otherwise have been. If it *wasn't* you, it still CAN be.

THE LAW OF ECONOMY

Within most of us there exists a natural desire for economy. We do not like to waste time, money, or energy, since wastefulness indicates a failure to perceive the real value of things.

Once you begin to attain a higher level of consciousness, you tend to bring the law of economy into more areas of your life. For the very first time, you will become aware of the needless drain that others have upon you. You will become less tolerant of their negativity, their need to burden you with their problems, their gloom-and-doom philosophies of life. You will find yourself conserving your own energies in new and different ways to prevent unnecessary dissipation. It all comes back to economy, something you have believed in all along, but never quite as intensely as you do now.

DISREGARDING OTHER PEOPLE'S OPINIONS

If you constantly feel pressure from other people, it is because you are giving them power over you. It is easy enough to become a victim, but not at all necessary. Are you presently concerned with what other people think? Assuming they think the worst, what is the real problem here? You cannot be hurt by what other people think and, in reality, you never are. The thoughts of others cannot hurt you. It is*your* thoughts about *their* thoughts that do the real damage.

UNDERSTANDING WILLPOWER

Do you take pride in having a lot of willpower? If so, you were undoubtedly raised to believe that this is an admirable quality. Actually, willpower is nothing special, since it is nothing more than the temporary domination of one desire over another.

All people with chronic weight problems have tremendous willpower. It is rare indeed when they are not exercising some power of will, even when they give in to occasional indulgences. One day, they are compelled to starve themselves, the next day they overeat. On each day, conflicting aspects of the human will are at work. The problem is that no long-term solution can ever be realized until the person acquires some form of higher knowledge.

Willpower that emanates from the true self is never in conflict with anything. Having weighed all the so-called pros and cons, the true self makes a realistic and totally objective choice—and that, as they say, is *that!*

PERCEPTION IS EVERYTHING

Do people constantly disappoint you? If so, do you think it is because of the way they *are,* or because of the way you *perceive* them?

Your disappointment is the result of your own false
assumptions. People who smile a lot are not necessarily
happy. Inside, they are often angry, bitter, or afraid.
Those who exhibit a calm and placid nature may well be
disguising some form of inner anguish that will eventually work its way to the surface. If we hope to see people
as they really are, we must first learn to understand ourselves. Gaining insight into our own thoughts and actions
will make the thoughts and actions of others increasingly
clear. Human nature being what it is, we have many
things in common, including an unfortunate tendency to
wear too many masks.

YOU DON'T HAVE TO SUFFER

Suffering of any kind tells us that we are out of harmony with the world. To be free of pain, we must allow
ourselves to see it through to the end, if only to see where
it leads. This must be done without anger, resistance, or
resentment. Suffering will always teach us, often by re-
veling the false foundations upon which we have chosen
to build our lives. It is unfortunate that so many would
rather live the lie than ever confront the truth, since only
the truth can end their suffering.

HANDLING REJECTION
AND RESENTMENT

When faced with another's anger or resentment, most
people will either retaliate in kind or attempt to appease
the other person's negative feelings. Both responses are
wrong. The wise individual will immediately ask himself

why he is allowing another person to dictate his responses when he could just as easily reject the other person's negative feelings.

Some people seek approval from others by doing things for others in order to get them to like them. As you already know, this only encourages people to take advantage because they sense your need of them.

If you are determined to garner the affection or respect of another, you must first prove yourself worthy of such feelings. What sort of person are *you* inclined to respect and admire? Has it ever been anyone who seemed desperate for your approval?

STARTING OVER— A NEW BEGINNING

How do you believe you would feel if today were your original birthday? That's right, the very first day of your life! You could enjoy it without prior conditioning, with total freshness and joy. There would be nothing to dread, nothing to feel defensive about. Not yet. For that matter, why should there *ever* be?

Today is all you have. If you are immersed in worrying about the future or in regretting the past, you are robbing yourself of the priceless present. It is unfortunate that so much attention is given over to the past and future, since neither time frame even exists! Only the present exists— and whatever you choose to do with it!